He flew a little farther and he came to another nest, high in a holly tree. He perched on the edge.

'Please may I come inside and rest?' he asked.

A soft grey wood pigeon was sitting on the nest. 'Can you say Coo! Coo! Coo!?' said the soft grey wood pigeon.

'No. I can only say Cheep! Cheep! Cheep!'

'Then you must go away. You don't belong to my family.'

He flew a little farther and he saw a hole in the trunk of an oak tree. Surely he could creep in and rest his tired wings. He put his head in the hole.

'Please may I come inside and rest?' he asked.

A brown owl with a hooked beak lived in the hole. 'Can you say Tu-whit! Tu-whoo!?' said the brown owl.

'No. I can only say Cheep! Cheep! Cheep!'

'Then you must go away. You don't belong to my family.'

He flew a little farther and he saw on the ground, by the edge of a pool, a nest of reeds and grasses. It looked so safe and comfortable. He hopped to the nest.

'Please may I come inside and rest?' he asked.

A wild duck with a flat yellow beak was sitting in the nest.

'Can you say Quack! Quack! Quack!?' said the wild duck.

'No. I can only say Cheep! Cheep! Cheep!'

'Then you must go away. You don't belong to my family.'

It was getting dark and the little sparrow could not fly any more. He was much too tired. He just went hop, hop along the ground. Soon he saw another bird hopping along.

'Do I belong to you?' asked the tired little sparrow. 'I can only say Cheep! Cheep! Cheep!'

'Of course you belong to me,' said the other bird. 'I am your mother and I have been looking for you all day. Perch on my back and I will carry you home.'

So the little sparrow perched on his mother's back and she carried him home to the nest in the ivy and he fell asleep under her warm wings.

From *Listen with Mother Tales*

The Tale of a Hazel Nut

BY ELIZABETH CLARK

Away in the country, in a place that I know, there is an oak wood. Under the oaks grow hazel nut trees and in spring-time every nut tree has bunches of little greeny yellow cat-kins, looking just like lambs' tails, that swing to and fro in the wind. There are tiny red flowers too, but they are so small that you can scarcely see them. When the lambs' tails and the flowers fall off the nuts begin to grow. They are very small indeed at first, like tiny green buds, but all through the summer-time they grow till they are as big as the tip of my middle finger. Some grow in pairs, some grow three to-gether. Some grow in bunches of four or five and some grow all alone. Every nut has a pale green cup, pointed and soft and frilly like the petals of a flower; and as the nuts grow larger they poke their tips out of their green cups and the sun and air ripen them and make them brown, as all good nuts should be.

The nut that this story is about grew all alone on the tip-top branch of a nut tree just on the edge of the wood. There were plenty of nuts on the other trees, in twos and threes and fours and fives. But our nut was the only one on the tree. The nut tree took great care of it and it grew smooth and plump in the sunshine and the wind and the rain. It was a very fine hazel nut and the tree was proud of it.

'I wonder what will happen to my fine big hazel nut?' said the nut tree to itself one day in July. 'It really is a beautiful nut, the best I have ever had. Well, we shall see,' said the tree.

21

And the hazel nut bobbed up and down in the wind and it sang to itself:

> 'What will happen?
> And what will you see?
> Here I am and here I'll be,
> On the tip-top branch
> Of the hazel tree.'

And it went on growing in the sunshine.

One day in August a big black Crow came flying past the wood. And the big black Crow said to himself: 'There's a fine large hazel nut.' And he took hold of the nut with his long strong beak and tried to pull it off the tree.

But the nut held tight and it said:

> 'Mr Crow, you may tweak
> With your long strong beak,
> But you can't tweak me
> Off the tip-top branch
> Of the hazel tree.'

So the Crow flew away and the nut bobbed up and down in the wind and it sang to itself:

> 'Here I am and here I'll be
> On the tip-top branch
> Of the hazel tree.'

And it went on growing in the sunshine.

One day in September a Squirrel looked down from the bough of an oak just above the nut tree and he said: 'That's a fine fat hazel nut. I must have it for my winter store-cupboard.'

So he bustled up the nut tree and he shook the tip-top
branch and he shook and he shook and he *shook*.

But the nut held tight and it said:

> 'I wouldn't go
> To please the Crow:
> And now Mr Squirrel,
> You may hustle
> You may bustle,
> But you can't shake me
> Off the tip-top branch
> Of the hazel tree.'

So the Squirrel went away and the nut bobbed up and down in the wind and it sang to itself:

> 'Here I am and here I'll be,
> On the tip-top branch
> Of the hazel tree.'

And it went on growing in the sunshine.

One day in October, Jenny Brown and her little brother Jack came trotting through the wood with long sticks to knock the nuts off the trees and a big basket to put them in; and they both said together, '*There's* a fine fat hazel nut.'

They tried to reach the nut with their long sticks; they poked and they beat. But only the leaves came fluttering down. The nut held tight and it said:

> 'I wouldn't go
> To please the Crow:
> The Squirrel couldn't take me,
> Although he tried to shake me:
> And you may beat and beat,
> But you won't have me to eat.
> For you can't knock me
> Off the tip-top branch
> Of the hazel tree.'

And it bobbed up and down in the wind and it sang to it-self:

> 'Here I am and here I'll be,
> On the tip-top branch
> Of the hazel tree.'

Nobody troubled it after that and it went on growing browner every day. The nights began to get cold and frosty.

The green leaves of the nut tree turned yellow and the little cup of the nut grew withered and brown.

And one day when most of the leaves of the nut tree had tumbled down after a very cold night, the nut said to itself in a sleepy voice:

> 'I wouldn't go
> To please the Crow:
> The Squirrel couldn't take me,
> Although he tried to shake me.
> The children couldn't beat me
> And knock me down to eat me.
> But now I want to sleep,
> Deep down deep,
> Down by the roots
> Of the hazel tree.'

And it nodded up and down till it nodded right off the tip-top branch and fell down, down, down to the ground. There it lay, all among the fallen leaves and the soft green moss. Some more leaves came floating down and covered it up snug and warm and it went to sleep for a long, long time.

But one day in spring-time a tiny green shoot peeped out of the earth and pushed up through the old dead leaves and the soft green moss. The little green shoot unfolded into two little green leaves; they were shaped like tiny nut-tree leaves. Then came another and another. And if you had poked down through the dead leaves and moss and earth till you came to the root of the little green thing you would have found that it was growing out of a nutshell. It was the shell of the fine big hazel nut.

And one day the big nut tree looked down and saw the tiny green thing with its tiny nut-tree leaves and the tree said: 'Why, here is my fine big hazel nut, growing into a dear little nut tree!'

And the tiny nut tree nodded and said:

> 'Yes, here I am and here I'll be,
> A nice little, strong little hazel tree.'

So there it is – still growing; and one day it will be a big nut tree and have hazel nuts of its own.

From *Tales for Jack and Jane*

The Tickle Rhyme

'Who's that tickling my back?' said the wall.
'Me,' said a small
caterpillar. 'I'm learning
to crawl.'

IAN SERRAILLIER

The Three Bears

TRADITIONAL

Once upon a time there were three Bears, a big Bear, a middle-sized Bear, and a teeny-weeny Bear. They all lived together in a little house in a wood.

One day the middle-sized Bear made some porridge and poured it into three plates, a big plate, a middle-sized plate, and a teeny-weeny plate. It was too hot to eat so the three Bears went out for a walk.

While they were out a little girl called Goldilocks came wandering through the wood. She had lost her way and when she saw the Bears' house, she knocked at the door, TAP, TAP, TAP. No one answered, so Goldilocks turned the handle and went in.

There was the table set for breakfast with the three plates of porridge.

'I'm so hungry!' said Goldilocks and took a spoonful of porridge from the big plate, but it was too salty. She took a spoonful from the middle-sized plate, but it was too lumpy. She took a spoonful from the teeny-weeny plate and it was just right – so she ate it all up.

'I'm so tired!' said Goldilocks and sat down in the big chair, but it was too hard. She sat down in the middle-sized chair, but it was too soft. She sat down in the teeny-weeny chair and it was just right – but the seat fell through.

Goldilocks climbed up the steep staircase to the bedroom. There were three beds – a big bed, a middle-sized bed, and a teeny-weeny bed.

Goldilocks tried to climb up on to the big bed, but it was too high. She scrambled on to the middle-sized bed, but it was too wide. She lay down on the teeny-weeny bed and it was just right, so she fell fast asleep.

At last the three Bears came home for breakfast and found the door open and the spoons in the porridge plates.

'Who's been eating *my* porridge?' growled the big Bear in a big voice.

'Who's been eating *my* porridge?' said the middle-sized Bear in a middle-sized voice.

'Who's been eating *my* porridge – and eaten it all up?' squeaked the teeny-weeny Bear in a teeny-weeny voice.

The Bears went to sit down. 'Who's been sitting in *my* chair?' growled the big Bear in a big voice.

'Who's been sitting in *my* chair?' said the middle-sized Bear in a middle-sized voice.

'Who's been sitting in *my* chair – and broken it to bits!' squeaked the teeny-weeny Bear in a teeny-weeny voice.

The three Bears climbed the steep stairs – THUMP! THUMP! STUMP! STUMP! PITTER-PATTER.

'Who's been climbing on *my* bed?' growled the big Bear in a big voice.

'Who's been lying on *my* bed?' said the middle-sized Bear in a middle-sized voice.

'Who's been lying on *my* bed – and is still there!' squeaked the teeny-weeny Bear in a teeny-weeny voice.

Goldilocks woke up with a start and when she saw the three Bears standing round the bed, she jumped up and ran down the stairs and away home to her mother.

So the three Bears went downstairs again to have their breakfast and the big Bear ate three plates of porridge and the middle-sized Bear ate two plates of porridge and the teeny-weeny Bear ate one HUGE plate of porridge covered all over with milk and sugar.

The Little Red Jersey

A Story for a Windy Day

BY LILIAN McCREA

Whish, whee! sang the wind, and the trees tossed their branches and shook off their leaves. 'It's snowing leaves,' laughed Timothy. 'Yes,' said Mummy, 'it is a windy day today. I think I'll wash your little red jersey; it will dry in no time at all.' 'Oh, yes,' said Timothy, 'and then I can wear it at my party tomorrow.' So Mummy washed the little red jersey, rub-a-dub-dub, scrub-a-dub-dub in lovely warm soapy water. Then she took it out into the garden and pegged it on the clothes line. 'There,' she said, 'you'll soon be dry now, Little Red Jersey.' And Mummy went back into the house and shut the door.

And the little red jersey out on the line began to dance and wave about. 'This is fun,' he said. 'Ha, ha!' laughed the wind, 'I want to have some fun too. Come on, I'll take you for a ride!' 'Oh, no,' cried the little red jersey. 'Oh, yes,' laughed the wind, and he tugged and tugged with all his might till down came the little red jersey, right off the line! 'Oh, dear,' he cried. 'Whatever's happening to me?' But before he had time to think, there he was sailing along in the sky, over the roof-tops and over the hedges, over the gardens and over the fields. On and on he sailed, on and on, until he came to a great brown oak-tree and there he stopped, caught in the middle of its twisted branches. 'Where do you think you're going, Little Red Jersey?' asked the oak-tree. 'I don't know,' cried the little red jersey.

'The wind blew me off the line and I must go home because Timothy wants to wear me tomorrow.' 'Well, you'll have to stay here now, until somebody helps you down,' said the oak-tree, 'because my arms are old and stiff, and I can't move them.' 'All right,' said the little red jersey, 'I'll have to watch for somebody to come and help me.'

Presently a brown cow came strolling along. 'Moo . . . Hello, Little Red Jersey,' she said. 'What are you doing up there?' 'Oh, please help me down, Mrs Cow,' cried the little red jersey. 'I must go home because Timothy wants to wear me tomorrow.' 'I would if I could,' said the brown cow, 'but I'm not tall enough to reach you.' And off she strolled.

Presently a black-and-white horse came trotting along. 'Neigh . . . Hello, Little Red Jersey,' he said. 'What are you doing up there?' 'Oh, please help me down, Mr Horse,' cried the little red jersey. 'I must go home because Timothy wants to wear me tomorrow.' 'I would if I could,' said the black-and-white horse, 'but I'm not tall enough to reach you.' And off he trotted.

Presently a frisky lamb came skipping along. 'Baa-aa-aa. Hello, Little Red Jersey,' he said. 'What are you doing up there?' 'Oh, please help me down, Baa-lamb,' cried the little red jersey. 'I must go home because Timothy wants to wear me tomorrow.' 'I would if I could,' said the little frisky lamb, 'but I'm not tall enough to reach you.' And off he skipped.

'Oh, dear,' cried the little red jersey. 'Nobody can help me. I'll have to stay here for ever and ever and ever.' 'Wait a minute,' said the oak-tree. 'Look who's coming now!' And the little red jersey looked and guess who he saw! A tiny grey squirrel scampering up the tree! 'Hello, Little Red Jersey, what are you doing up here? Are you looking for

acorns, like me?' 'Oh, no,' cried the little red jersey, 'I'm just waiting for someone to help me down because I want to go home. Will you help me?' 'Of course I will,' said the squirrel and he pushed the little red jersey off the tree! And before he had time to say 'thank you' the wind came along and caught the little red jersey again. 'Oh, Mr Wind, please take me home. Timothy wants to wear me tomorrow,' he cried. 'All right,' laughed the wind, 'I was only having a little fun. I'll have you home again in exactly one minute.'

And the little red jersey went sailing home in the sky, over the fields and over the gardens, over the hedges and over the roof-tops, until he came to his very own garden. 'Can you peg me back on the line, Mr Wind?' he asked. 'I want to get dry.' 'No,' said the wind. 'because I haven't any hands. But I'll leave you here on the door-step and Timothy's Mummy will find you.'

And when Mummy opened the door, there was the little red jersey on the door-step. 'Good gracious!' she said, lifting him up, 'have you blown off the line? Why, you're all black; I'll have to wash you all over again!' And she took the little red jersey into the house and rub-a-dub-dub, scrub-a-dub-dub, she washed him again in lovely warm soapy water. 'There!' she said, 'I think I'll dry you by the fire this time, and you won't blow away again.' And she spread the little red jersey on a clothes-horse in front of the warm glowing fire. And oh, how happy he was! 'Now I'll be ready for Timothy to wear at his party tomorrow,' he said. And he stretched himself out to dry his very best.

From *Stories to Tell in the Nursery School*

Finger Play

Mousie come a-creeping, creeping.
(*Close the fist and push the first finger of
the other hand through it slowly*)
Mousie come a-peeping, peeping.
(*Waggle finger*)
Mousie said, 'I'd like to stay
But I haven't time today.'
Mousie popped into his hole
(*Draw finger back quickly*)
And said 'Achoo! Achoo!
I've got a cold!'

LILIAN McCREA

Mother Hen

BY LILIAN McCREA

Mother Hen was sitting on her nest in a corner of the barn. Her nest was a wooden box filled with soft brown hay. And in the box, on top of the soft brown hay and underneath Mother Hen were ten brown eggs! Mother Hen was sitting on her ten brown eggs to keep them warm until her baby chickens came out.

Every morning the farmer came into the barn carrying a dish of corn and a basin of water. And he put them down on the floor just beside Mother Hen's nest. 'Now, Mother Hen,' he said, 'you haven't far to go for your breakfast!' 'Cluck, cluck. Thank you!' said Mother Hen, and she flew off her nest and pecked up the corn, and drank a little water. And in just a minute she was back again in her warm nest sitting on her ten brown eggs.

And every day Winkie, the farmer's black-and-white cat, came softly into the barn on her four white feet, and said, 'Mew, mew. It is sunny and warm in the farm-yard today. Aren't you coming out, Mother Hen?' But 'Cluck, cluck,' said Mother Hen. 'I can't come out, I must sit on my eggs and keep them warm.' And she fluffed out her feathers and settled herself again on her nest of soft brown hay, where she cuddled her ten brown eggs.

And every day, Bob, the farmer's big black dog, came into the barn, pit-pat on his four black feet, and said, 'Bow-wow. It's a fine day for a walk. Aren't you coming out, Mother Hen?' But 'Cluck, cluck,' said Mother Hen. 'I can't come out. I must sit on my eggs and keep them warm.' And she fluffed out her feathers and settled herself again on her nest of soft brown hay, where she cuddled her ten brown eggs.

And when Strawberry, the farmer's red-and-white cow, came into the barn to be milked, she said, 'Moo-oo. The grass in the fields is juicy and green. Aren't you coming out, Mother Hen?' But 'Cluck, cluck,' said Mother Hen. 'I can't come out. I must sit on my eggs and keep them warm.' And she fluffed out her feathers, and settled herself again on her nest of soft brown hay, where she cuddled her ten brown eggs.

And at night-time when Nobby, the farmer's big white horse, came into the barn to sleep, he said, 'Neigh-eigh-eigh. You haven't been out all day, Mother Hen!' 'Cluck, cluck,' said Mother Hen. 'I couldn't come out today, and I can't come out tomorrow. I must sit on my eggs and keep them warm.' And she fluffed out her feathers and settled herself again on her nest of soft brown hay, where she cuddled her ten brown eggs.

And Mother Hen sat on her nest of soft brown hay, and cuddled her ten brown eggs for a very long time. Days and days went by, but still she sat on her nest. Then one day, Mother Hen heard a little noise underneath her that went cr-ick! cr-ack! ... What do you think had happened? – a little yellow chicken had pecked open its brown egg and come out! 'Cluck! cluck!' said Mother Hen. And just as she said that, cr-ick! cr-ack! went another brown egg and out came another little yellow chicken! And cr-ick! cr-ack! went another! and another! and another! until all Mother Hen's brown eggs were broken, and in her nest were ten yellow chickens! 'Cluck, cluck. Come under my wings,' said Mother Hen, and she spread her big brown wings over her baby chickens. And 'Peep, peep,' they said, as they cuddled close to her warm brown body.

Then, in a little while, Mother Hen said, 'Cluck, cluck! Come along now. The sun is shining, so we'll go for a walk.' And Mother Hen got down off her nest, and her ten baby chickens came after her, calling 'Peep, peep. We're coming.'

Out into the sunny farm-yard went Mother Hen, with her ten baby chickens behind her. Winkie, the farmer's black-and-white cat, was sitting in the sun washing her face. But when Mother Hen came along she stopped . . . and looked . . . 'Mew! mew!' she said. 'Are those your yellow chickens, Mother Hen?' 'Cluck, cluck. All mine,' said Mother Hen. 'Mew, mew. I must go and tell Bob,' said Winkie. And away she ran on her four white feet to Bob, the farmer's big black dog. 'Mew, mew,' she said. 'Do you know, Mother

Hen has ten baby chickens all her own!' 'Bow-wow!' said Bob. 'I must go and tell Strawberry.' And off he ran on his four black feet to Strawberry, the farmer's red-and-white cow. 'Bow-wow,' he said. 'Do you know, Mother Hen has ten baby chickens all her own!' 'Moo-oo,' said Strawberry. 'I must go and tell Nobby.' And away she went on her red-and-white legs to Nobby, the farmer's big white horse. 'Moo-oo,' she said. 'Do you know, Mother Hen has ten baby chickens all her own!' 'Neigh-eigh-eigh!' said Nobby. 'Let's go and see!'

And Winkie and Bob and Strawberry and Nobby all went to the farm-yard, and there, walking about in the sun, was brown Mother Hen with her ten yellow chickens behind her. 'Mew, mew,' said Winkie. 'Bow-wow,' said Bob. 'Moo-oo,' said Strawberry. 'Neigh-eigh-eigh,' said Nobby. 'We like your yellow chickens, Mother Hen!' Then 'Cluck, cluck,' said Mother Hen. And off she went, with her ten baby chickens behind her, calling 'Peep, peep, we're coming.'

From *Nursery World*

The Gingerbread Boy

TRADITIONAL

Once upon a time there was a little old man and a little old woman. They had no children but lived all alone in their little wooden house.

One day the little old woman made a little boy out of gingerbread. His nose was a currant and two currants made his eyes. He had a row of currant buttons down his coat. The little old woman put the gingerbread boy in the oven to bake. Then she went on with her work.

When she came back into the kitchen, she heard a tiny voice calling, 'Let me out! Let me out!'

The moment she opened the oven door, out popped the little gingerbread boy and skipped across the kitchen floor. Away he went down the street and after him ran the little old man and the little old woman. 'Stop, little gingerbread boy!' they cried.

But the little gingerbread boy said:

> 'Run, run, as fast as you can,
>   You can't catch me,
>   I'm the gingerbread man.'

Along the road he met a cow. 'Stop, gingerbread boy!' mooed the cow. 'I should like to eat you.'

But the gingerbread boy cried, 'I've run away from a little old man and a little old woman, and I can run away from you, I can.'

'Run, run, as fast as you can,
You can't catch me,
I'm the gingerbread man.'

And the cow could not catch him.

A horse came out of a gate on to the road. 'Stop, ginger-bread boy!' neighed the horse. 'I should like to eat you.'

The gingerbread boy ran faster than ever and cried, 'I have run away from a little old man and a little old woman and a cow. I can run away from you too, I can.'

'Run, run, as fast as you can,
You can't catch me,
I'm the gingerbread man.'

And the horse could not catch him.

'No one can catch me,' said the little gingerbread boy. 'I can run faster than anyone, I can.'

Soon after he met a sly old fox. 'Wait, little gingerbread boy,' said the fox. 'I should like to talk to you.'

But the little gingerbread boy cried, 'I have run away from a little old man and a little old woman and a cow and a horse. I can run away from you too, I can.'

'Run, run, as fast as you can,
You can't catch me,
I'm the gingerbread man.'

And he kept on running – but so did the fox. The little gingerbread boy ran faster – but so did the fox. Soon they came to a river.

The little gingerbread boy could not swim, so he had to stop at last. The fox caught up to him and said, 'Jump on my tail and I will take you over the river.'

The gingerbread boy got on to the fox's tail and the fox began to swim across the river.

'You had better get on to my back,' said the fox. 'The water is deep.'

The gingerbread boy got on to the fox's back.

'You will get wet,' said the Fox. 'You had better get on to my nose.'

The gingerbread boy got on to the fox's nose.

The fox reached the other side of the river and climbed out on to the bank. He tossed the gingerbread boy into the air and snap! he caught him in his mouth.

'Dear me,' said the little gingerbread boy, 'I'm a quarter gone.'

'Dear me,' said the little gingerbread boy, 'I'm half gone.'

'Dear me,' said the little gingerbread boy, 'I'm three-quarters gone.'

And that was all he said for he was *all* gone.

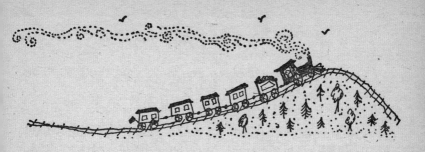

Playing at Trains

Puff, puff, puff!
Puff, puff, puff!
That's the way
We play at trains –
Puff, puff, puff! . . .

Sh-sh-sh!
Sh-sh-sh!
That's the way
We go up hills –
Sh-sh-sh!

S-s-s!
S-s-s!
That's the way
We let off steam –
S-s-s!

Stop, stop, stop!
Stop, stop, stop!
Don't you see
The signal's up?
Stop, stop, stop!

RODNEY BENNETT

The Very First Story

BY DOROTHY EDWARDS

A very long time ago, when I was a little girl, I didn't have a naughty little sister at all. I was a child *all on my own*. I had a father and a mother of course, but I hadn't any other little brothers or sisters – I was *quite alone*.

I was a very lucky little girl because I had a dear grannie and a dear grandad and lots of kind aunts and uncles to make a fuss of me. They played games with me, and gave me toys and took me for walks, and bought me ice-creams and told me stories, but I *hadn't* got a little sister.

Well now, one day, when I was a child on my own, I went to stay with my kind godmother-aunt in the country. My kind godmother-aunt was very good to me. She took me out every day to see the farm animals and to pick flowers, and she read stories to me, and let me cook little cakes and jam tarts in her oven, and I was very, very happy. I didn't want to go home one bit.

Then, one day, my godmother-aunt said, 'Here is a letter from your father, and *what* do you think he says?'

My aunt was smiling and smiling. 'What do you think he says?' she asked. 'He says that you have a little baby sister waiting for you at home!'

I *was* excited! I said, 'I think I had better go home AT ONCE, don't you?' and my kind godmother-aunt said, 'I think you had indeed.' And she took me home that very very day!

My aunt took me on a train and a bus and another bus, and then I was home!

And, do you know, before I'd even got indoors, I heard a waily-waily noise coming from the house, and my god-mother-aunt said, 'That is your new sister.'

'Waah-waah,' my little sister was saying, 'waah-waah.'

I was surprised to think that such a very new child could make so much noise, and I ran straight indoors and straight upstairs and straight into my mother's bedroom. And there was my good kind mother sitting up in bed smiling and smiling, and there, in a cot that used to be my old cot, was my new cross little sister crying and crying!

My mother said, 'Sh-sh, baby, here is your big sister come to see you.' My mother lifted my naughty little sister out of the cot, and my little sister stopped crying at once.

My mother said, 'Come and look.'

My little sister was wrapped up in a big woolly white shawl, and my mother undid the shawl and there was my little sister! When my mother put her down on the bed, my little sister began to CRY AGAIN.

She was a little, little red baby, crying and crying.

'Waah-waah, waah-waah,' – like that. Isn't it a nasty noise?

My little sister had tiny hands, and tiny little feet. She went on crying and crying, and curling up her toes, and beating with her arms in a very cross way.

My mother said, 'She likes being lifted up and cuddled. She is a very good baby when she is being cuddled and fussed but when I put her down she cries and cries. She is an *artful pussy*,' my mother said.

I was very sorry to see my little sister crying, and I was disappointed because I didn't want a crying little sister very much, but I went and looked at her. I looked at her little red face and her little screwed up eyes and her little crying mouth and then I said, 'Don't cry baby, don't cry baby.'

And, do you know, when I said, 'Don't cry baby,' my little sister *stopped crying*, really stopped crying at once. For me! Because *I* told her to. She opened her eyes and she looked and looked and she didn't cry any more.

My mother said, ' Just fancy! She must know you are her own big sister! She has stopped crying.'

I was pleased to think that my little sister had stopped crying because she knew I was her big sister, and I put my finger on my sister's tiny, tiny hand and my little sister caught hold of my finger tight with her little curly fingers.

My mother said I could hold my little sister on my lap if I was careful. So I sat down on a chair and my godmother-aunt put my little sister on to my lap, and I held her very carefully; and my little sister didn't cry at all. She went to sleep like a good baby.

And do you know, she was so small and so sweet and she held my finger so tightly with her curly little fingers that I loved her and loved her and although she often cried after that I never minded it a bit, because I knew how nice and cuddly she could be when she was good!

From *More Naughty Little Sister Stories*

The Bear Who Wanted to be a Bird

BY ADELE AND CATEAU DE LEEUW

There was once a little black bear who wanted to be a bird. He wished it so hard, and thought about it so much, that finally he decided he *was* one.

Going through the forest one day he saw some birds high up in a tree. 'Hello,' he said. 'I'm a bird, too.'

The birds laughed at him. '*You're* not a bird,' they said. 'Birds have beaks.'

The little black bear scurried through the forest until he found a thin piece of wood that had a point. He tied it to his muzzle and hurried back to the tree where the birds sat. 'See,' he cried, looking up, 'I have a beak!'

'Just the same,' they said, 'you're not a bird. Birds have feathers.'

So the little black bear ran as fast as he could out of the forest and found a chicken yard. There were lots of feathers lying on the ground. He picked them up and went back to the forest. There he sat down on some pine needles and stuck the feathers all over his head and his shoulders and down his front legs. Then he went to the tree where the birds sat and cried happily, 'I have feathers, too. See, I'm a bird.'

But the birds only laughed at him. 'You're not a bird,' they said. 'Don't you know that birds sing?'

The little black bear felt sad, but not for long. He remembered that deep in the forest was a house where a singing teacher lived. He went there and knocked on the door. 'Please teach me to sing,' he begged. 'I *must* learn to sing.'

'It's most unusual,' said the singing teacher. 'But I will try. I have a wonderful system. Come in. Open your mouth. Now follow me – do, re, mi, re, do . . . do, re, mi, re, do.'

The little black bear practised and practised and practised for a whole week, and then, feeling that he was very good indeed, he hurried back to the tree where the birds were.

'Listen,' he cried. 'I can sing, too.' And he opened his mouth very wide, and in a deep voice sang, 'Do, re, mi, re, do . . . do, re, mi, re, do.'

The birds laughed harder than ever. 'You're not a bird,' they told him. 'Birds fly.'

The little black bear said, 'I can fly, too.' He lifted first one foot, all covered with feathers, and then the other, and then hopped up and down, lifting both together. But he did not fly.

'I must get higher off the ground,' he said. 'Watch me.' So he went to a big rock near by and climbed up on it, and looked over the edge. The ground seemed very far away. 'But,' he thought, 'maybe if I take a running start, and don't look down, it will be all right.' So he backed off, closed his eyes, ran as fast as he could to the edge of the rock, lifted his feet, flapped them – and fell, with a loud smack, on his little behind on the ground.

He opened his eyes, and felt the tears coming. It hurt where he had fallen. His beak had slipped off; feathers were lying all over the ground.

The little birds laughed and laughed, high up in the tree, and then they all flew away together.

'You're not a bird,' they called, and it floated back to him on the wind. 'You're not a bird, you're a bear.'

He picked himself up and walked slowly through the forest. He felt very bad, and everything ached.

He rubbed his muzzle, and was glad that the clumsy beak wasn't tied to it any more. He picked the rest of the feathers off himself, and his fur felt very soft and furry. He found a bush with some beautiful red berries on it. They looked good, and he went over and stripped some off and ate them. They were delicious – much, much nicer than the worms that birds had to eat – and he ran his tongue around his black muzzle and pulled off another bunch.

After a while he met another bear, just about his size, coming towards him in the forest. 'Hello,' said the other bear.

'Wuf, wuf,' said the little black bear. And he thought, 'I like the sound of that. It's much better than having to sing do, re, mi, re, do in a deep voice.'

'Come and see what *I've* found,' his new friend said.

He led him to a big tree and climbed it. 'Follow me,' he said, and the little black bear did. Up in the first crotch was a bees' nest and a big comb of honey.

'Oh,' said the little black bear, 'what a wonderful find!' He dipped his paw in the honeycomb and licked it. Then he dipped it in again and licked it once more.

'I'm *glad* I'm a bear,' he said. 'Who would want to be a bird, anyhow?'

From *Read Me Another Story*

The Rainy Morning

BY EDITH FRASER

David John woke up one morning, stretched until his toes nearly touched the bottom of the bed, and then suddenly sat up.

'The swing!' he cried, 'this is the day for trying the new swing!' And he jumped out of bed, washed and dressed very quickly, and ran downstairs.

'Daddy, can I try the new swing today?' he shouted, and danced up and down with excitement.

'Well, I expect the cement is quite dry by now,' said Daddy. 'But look out of the window.'

And then, for the first time, David John looked.

It was raining. It was *pouring*! The raindrops were bouncing up from the path and dashing against the window as though they were trying to get in.

'My goodness gracious me!' gasped David John, and he was so disappointed that he almost felt like crying.

'Never mind, old chap! It's sure to clear up before long,'

said Daddy, and Mummy let him have golden syrup on his porridge to help cheer him up.

But although he made a lovely pattern with the runny syrup, he still felt very sad, because he had been looking forward to the new swing so much.

And after breakfast it was just as bad. The rain still came pouring down, and there wasn't a bit of blue sky to be seen anywhere.

'Cheer up, David John,' smiled his Mummy, 'the time will soon pass if you find yourself something nice to do.'

'But there *isn't* anything nice to do!' pouted David John.

'Then would you like to help me?' asked Mummy.

'But that's *work*!' cried David John, 'and I don't want to work.'

'Well, work is fun too,' said Mummy, 'and I've got such a lot to do this morning.'

'Oh, all right, then,' muttered David John grumpily.

'That's the way,' smiled Mummy, pretending not to notice. 'Let's start by cleaning out the drawer where all the knives and forks go. It's in a dreadful muddle – just look!' And so it was. The big spoons were all mixed up with the teaspoons, some of the forks were the wrong way round, and, worse still, some of the knives were upside down.

It was still raining, so David John took all the things out of the drawer and began to arrange them in their proper places. This was a job David John liked, and he made the drawer look very tidy.

'That does look nice!' said Mummy. 'And now I've finished washing up, let's go and make the beds!'

'But I don't *want* to make beds,' grumbled David John.

'Well, they won't be very comfortable to sleep in if we don't,' answered his Mummy.

So, since the rain was still pouring down, he helped to bump up the pillows and tuck in the sheets and blankets.

'You *are* being a help this morning,' said Mummy. 'Now I shall have time to do some cooking. Come and help me!'

'But I don't really want to do cooking,' said David John, although it was much more fun than making beds. He looked through the window, and it was still raining.

So he greased all the little bun tins, and then Mummy began to fill them up.

'Can I clean out the bowl?' he asked. 'Leave me a nice lot, won't you?'

'Well, I won't scrape the bowl out very hard,' chuckled

Mummy. So he got himself a teaspoon from the tidy drawer, sat on the stool, and cleaned that bowl out so well that it didn't really need washing.

'Now for some tarts,' said Mummy, 'and you can put the jam in.'

David John glanced at the window. It was still raining.

So he put a spoonful of jam in every tart, right in the middle, blackcurrant jam in one lot, and raspberry in the others.

'I've got a bit of pastry left over,' said Mummy. 'Would you like to make a pastry man?'

And this time David John didn't even look at the window, because this was a fine job. He stood on the stool, and first he made a little ball for the man's head, then a big one for his body. Next he made two short sausages for his arms, and two long ones for his legs. Then he stuck them all together, and laid the man on the tin.

'That's good!' said Mummy. 'Now what about some currants for his eyes?'

'Ooh yes! and for buttons!' cried David John.

So he put in two black eyes, and as many buttons as he could find room for, all down the front, and then Mummy put the tin in the oven.

'While it cooks, let's do the dining-room. You can push the carpet-sweeper,' said Mummy.

David John used both hands, pushed hard, and picked up every crumb, and this time he quite forgot about the rain.

'Is my man done yet, Mummy?' he asked.

'Let's go and see,' said Mummy. She opened the oven door very carefully, and there was the pastry man, cooked exactly right. At that very moment there was a knock at the back door, and there stood Patsy Jane, who lived at the corner house.

'Aren't you coming out?' she asked. 'It's stopped raining.'

'My goodness gracious me! So it has!' cried David John. 'And I've been so busy that I didn't even notice!'

'Work isn't so bad, is it?' smiled Mummy.

'Why, I *like* work!' cried David John. 'And now, can we have a swing on my new swing?'

So they ate the pastry man while Mummy wiped the swing seat dry, and then they took turns.

Chacky the blackbird flew down on to the apple tree and began to sing. The sun came out and shone on all the wet leaves until they sparkled. A skylark rose up from the meadow, and the lambs were calling to their mothers on the hill.

And as David John swung higher and higher and higher, he sang:

'Here I go up in the swing so high,
Till the tips of my toes almost touch the sky!'
because he felt so happy.

From *David John*

Finger Play

Two fat gentlemen met in a lane,
    (*Thumbs*)
Bowed most politely, bowed once again,
How d'you do,
  How d'you do,
    How d'you do again?

Two thin ladies met in a lane, *etc.*
    (*Forefingers*)
Two tall policemen, *etc.*
    (*Middle fingers*)
Two little schoolboys, *etc.*
    (*Fourth fingers*)

Two little babies, *etc.*
    (*Little fingers*)

KATHLEEN BARTLETT

Mouse and the Little Blue Coat

BY WINIFRED G. LOVELL

A little old man had a little black dog, so small that she was called Mouse. Mouse loved to go hunting. She trotted through the wood on her tiny little feet, waving her tail like a feather behind her, hoping to find a baby rabbit. Her long nose went sniffing and snuffing under the bushes, through the bracken, round the tree stumps, and along by the hedge. She had never caught a rabbit, but every day she hurried through the wood looking for a rabbit-hole.

One winter day, Mouse trotted along the path, sniffing and snuffing, when all at once she smelt the lovely smell of bunny. She was so excited that she squealed and squealed with joy, and ran faster and faster, under the bushes, through the bracken, round the tree stumps, along by the hedge, and there, right in front of her, was a hole – a rabbit-hole!

It was not a very big hole, but Mouse was a very small dog. Down the hole she went, through a long tunnel, and then, with a loud bark, she stopped. In front of her was a great, big, brown rabbit. Mouse barked at him, but the rabbit didn't run away! He waggled his long ears, and wrinkled his soft nose, wuffle, wuffle, wuffle. Mouse barked as loudly as she could, 'wouf, wouf, wouf,' but the rabbit just sat and looked at her.

'Why don't you run away?' said Mouse. 'I can't catch you if you don't run away.'

'Why do you want to catch me? said Mr Rabbit.

'I don't exactly know,' said Mouse. 'But rabbits always run away from dogs, and dogs always chase them. Aren't you frightened?'

'Well, no, I'm not frightened,' said Mr Rabbit. 'You see, you are such a very little dog.'

'Hear me bark,' said Mouse, and she barked and barked and BARKED.

'Oh, my scut and whiskers! Whatever is that noise?' said a voice. 'Be quiet, or you will wake my babies!' And there was *Mrs* Rabbit.

'Oh, it's you, is it? I've often seen you in the wood. Stop that noise and come and see my babies.'

She led Mouse along another tunnel, and there, all in a row, were five baby rabbits, as snug as could be, and all fast asleep.

'Well, now you know the way, you must come again,' she said. 'Good-bye.'

The next day, when Mouse went out with the little old man, she found that the world had turned white, for snow had fallen in the night.

'We must buy you a coat,' said the little old man, 'a coat to keep you warm and dry.'

So the little old man bought a nice warm coat for his little black dog. It was blue with red braid all round. It fastened round her neck with a little strap and a buckle and underneath her tummy with two straps, and two buckles.

'There,' said the little old man, as he strapped on the blue coat with red braid all round, 'now you'll be warm and dry.'

Mouse growled and growled. The coat tickled her neck and tickled her tummy. It rubbed against her little legs, and she didn't like it at all. She wriggled and wriggled, trying to get out of it, but the little blue coat with red braid all round fitted very well, and she couldn't get even one little paw through the strap.

The little old man sat down by the fire and went to sleep.

Mouse crept out of the door and down the path to the wood, her little feet making tiny footprints in the snow, her tail waving like a black feather behind her. She sniffed and snuffed under the bushes, through the bracken, round the tree stumps and along the hedge, until she came to the rabbit-hole. She gave one little bark, just for politeness, and scurried down the tunnel.

'Oh, my scut and whiskers!' said Mrs Rabbit. 'Who is this? Why, it's Mouse! I didn't know you in your skating suit.'

'It isn't a skating suit,' said Mouse, 'and I don't like it at all. It tickles me and it is too tight. I can hardly breathe, and I can't get it off. Wouldn't you like it, Mrs Rabbit? It would make a lovely blanket for your babies.'

'So it would,' said Mrs Rabbit. 'Help her out of it, Mr Rabbit.'

So Mr Rabbit tugged at the buckles with his sharp teeth, and one by one he undid the straps. Off came the coat. Mrs Rabbit laid it very gently over her sleeping babies.

'Don't they look sweet?' she said. 'And won't it keep them warm? I've always had a fancy for red and blue.'

Very happily Mouse said 'Good-bye' and trotted home.

The little old man looked at her. 'Where is your coat?' he asked.

'Wouf,' said Mouse, and waved her tail like a feather.

'Come and find it,' said the little old man, and he went down through the snowy wood, with Mouse trotting at his heels. And they looked and they looked, but the little old man never saw the little blue coat with red braid all round again. But Mouse saw it, very often!

From *A Baker's Dozen of Stories for Telling*

Milly-Molly-Mandy Goes to a Party

BY JOYCE LANKESTER BRISLEY

Once upon a time something very nice happened in the village where Milly-Molly-Mandy and her Father and Mother and Grandpa and Grandma and Uncle and Aunty lived. Some ladies clubbed together to give a party to all the children in the village, and of course Milly-Molly-Mandy was invited.

Little-friend-Susan had an invitation too, and Billy Blunt (whose father kept the corn-shop where Milly-Molly-Mandy's Uncle got his chicken-feed), and Jilly, the little niece of Miss Muggins (who kept the shop where Milly-Molly-Mandy's Grandma bought her knitting-wool), and lots of others whom Milly-Molly-Mandy knew.

It was exciting.

Milly-Molly-Mandy had not been to a real party for a long time, so she was very pleased and interested when Mother said, 'Well, Milly-Molly-Mandy, you must have a proper new dress for a party like this. We must think what we can do.'

So Mother and Grandma and Aunty thought together for a bit, and then Mother went to the big wardrobe and rummaged in her bottom drawer until she found a most beautiful white silk scarf, which she had worn when she was married to Father, and it was just wide enough to be made into a party frock for Milly-Molly-Mandy.

Then Grandma brought out of her best handkerchief-box a most beautiful lace handkerchief, which would just cut into a little collar for the neck of the party frock.

And Aunty brought out of her small top drawer some most beautiful pink ribbon, all smelling of lavender – just enough to make into a sash for the party frock.

And then Mother and Aunty set to work to cut and stitch at the party frock, while Milly-Molly-Mandy jumped up and down and handed pins when they were wanted.

The next day Father came in with a paper parcel for Milly-Molly-Mandy bulging in his coat-pocket, and when Milly-Molly-Mandy unwrapped it she found the most beautiful little pair of red shoes inside!

And then Grandpa came in and held out his closed hand to Milly-Molly-Mandy, and when Milly-Molly-Mandy got his fingers open she found the most beautiful little coral necklace inside!

And then Uncle came in, and he said to Milly-Molly-Mandy, 'What have I done with my handkerchief?' And he felt in all his pockets. 'Oh, here it is!' And he pulled out the most beautiful little handkerchief with a pink border, which of course Milly-Molly-Mandy just knew was meant for her, and she wouldn't let Uncle wipe his nose on it, which he pretended he was going to do!

Milly-Molly-Mandy was so pleased she hugged everybody in turn – Father, Mother, Grandpa, Grandma, Uncle, and Aunty.

At last the great day arrived, and little-friend-Susan, in her best spotted dress and silver bangle, called for Milly-Molly-Mandy, and they went together to the village institute, where the party was to be.

There was a lady outside who welcomed them in, and there were more ladies inside who helped them to take their things off. And everywhere looked so pretty, with garlands of coloured paper looped from the ceiling, and everybody in their best clothes.

Most of the boys and girls were looking at a row of toys on the mantelpiece, and a lady explained that they were all prizes, to be won by the children who got the most marks in the games they were going to have. There was a lovely fairy doll and a big Teddy Bear and a picture book and all sorts of things.

And at the end of the row was a funny little white cotton-wool rabbit with a pointed paper hat on his head. And directly Milly-Molly-Mandy saw him she wanted him dreadfully badly, more than any of the other things.

Little-friend-Susan wanted the picture book, and Miss Muggins' niece, Jilly, wanted the fairy doll. But the black, beady eyes of the little cotton-wool rabbit gazed so wistfully at Milly-Molly-Mandy that she determined to try ever so hard in all the games and see if she could win him.

Then the games began, and they were fun! They had a spoon-and-potato race, and musical chairs, and putting the tail on the donkey blindfold, and all sorts of guessing-games.

And then they had supper – bread-and-butter with coloured hundreds-and-thousands sprinkled on, and red jellies and yellow jellies, and cakes with icing and cakes with cherries, and lemonade in red glasses.

It was quite a proper party.

And at the end the names of prize-winners were called out, and the children had to go up and receive their prizes.

And what do you think Milly-Molly-Mandy got?

Why, she had tried so hard to win the little cotton-wool rabbit that she won first prize instead, and got the lovely fairy doll!

And Miss Muggins' niece Jilly, who hadn't won any of the games, got the little cotton-wool rabbit with the sad, beady eyes – for do you know, the cotton-wool rabbit was only the booby prize, after all!

It was a lovely fairy doll, but Milly-Molly-Mandy was sure Miss Muggins' Jilly wasn't loving the booby rabbit as it ought to be loved, for its beady eyes did look so sad, and when she got near Miss Muggins' Jilly she stroked the booby rabbit, and Miss Muggins' Jilly stroked the fairy doll's hair.

Then Milly-Molly-Mandy said, 'Do you love the fairy doll more than the booby rabbit?'

And Miss Muggins' Jilly said, 'I should think so!'

So Milly-Molly-Mandy ran up to the lady who had given the prizes, and asked if she and Miss Muggins' Jilly might exchange prizes, and the lady said, 'Yes, of course.'

So Milly-Molly-Mandy and the booby rabbit went home together to the nice white cottage with the thatched roof, and Father and Mother and Grandpa and Grandma and Uncle and Aunty all liked the booby rabbit very much indeed.

And do you know, one day one of his little bead eyes dropped off, and when Mother had stuck it on again with a dab of glue, his eyes didn't look a bit sad any more, but almost as happy as Milly-Molly-Mandy's own!

From *Milly-Molly-Mandy Stories*

'Who's that ringing at the front door bell?'
    Miau! Miau! Miau!
'I'm a little Pussy Cat and I'm not very well!'
    Miau! Miau! Miau!
'Then rub your nose in a bit of mutton fat.'
    Miau! Miau! Miau!
'For that's the way to cure a little Pussy Cat.'
    Miau! Miau! Miau!

D'ARCY W. THOMPSON

The Little Red Hen

TRADITIONAL

There was once a little Red Hen who lived all by herself in a pretty little house with red and white checked curtains at the window. She swept and dusted and polished until everything shone and at night she sat in her rocking-chair and stitched and mended. She was as happy as the day was long.

Nearby in a dark and dirty house lived Mr and Mrs Fox. Mr Fox had tried many times to catch the little Red Hen but she was always too clever for him.

One day Mr Fox said to his wife: 'Put a big pot on the fire and have the water boiling and I will bring you a fine dinner.' He took a sack and set out for the little Red Hen's house and there he hid in the currant bushes.

By and by out came the little Red Hen, leaving the door ajar. She was wearing a little red and white apron with a pocket which held her scissors and needle and thread. She began to fill a basket with sticks for the fire.

The moment her back was turned, the wicked old Fox slipped in at the open door and hid behind the chair. In came the little Red Hen – and out jumped the fox from his hiding place.

'SQUAWK!' cried the little Red Hen and, dropping her basket, she flew up on to the beam across the ceiling. She fluffed out her feathers and said: 'You can't catch me, Mr Fox!'

'Oh, can't I?' growled Mr Fox and he began to run round

and round after his own tail. Faster and faster he twirled until the little Red Hen was so dizzy that she fell right off the beam on to the floor.

SNAP! The bad old Fox popped her into his sack and started off for home.

It was a hot day and the Fox was feeling dizzy too, so he stopped to rest under a tree. Soon he was snoring BR-R-R.

As soon as she heard him snore, the little Red Hen took her scissors out of her pocket and SNIP, SNIP, she cut a hole in the sack big enough for her to crawl through.

'BR-R-R-R,' snored the Fox.

Then that clever little Hen fetched a large stone and pushed it through the hole in the sack.

'BR-R-R-R,' snored the Fox.

The little Red Hen took out her needle and thread and sewed up the hole neatly.

'BR-R-R-R,' snored the Fox.

Away ran the little Red Hen, away to her pretty little house. There she locked the door, made herself a cup of tea, and sat down in her rocking-chair to rest.

At last the old Fox woke up, put his sack over his shoulder and went on home. The sack seemed very heavy. 'How fat the little Red Hen must be!' he thought. 'She will make a fine dinner.'

'Here you are, wife,' he said to Mrs Fox. 'I have caught the little Red Hen at last. Is the pot boiling? Hold up the lid and I'll drop her in.'

Mrs Fox lifted the lid and Mr Fox opened the mouth of the sack and tipped out – A STONE!

PLONK! The big stone fell in the boiling water and

splashed it all over Mr and Mrs Fox. And that was the end of *them* and a good thing too.

But the little Red Hen lived happily ever after in her pretty little house.

Henry the Postman

BY DORA THATCHER

It was the day before Christmas Eve, and it had snowed and snowed for three whole days and two whole nights. Outside the hangar where Henry lived the aerodrome was covered with a thick white blanket of snow. It was very quiet, because the snow was too thick on the runways for the aeroplanes to fly.

The airliners and the big cargo planes that lived in the hangar with Henry were having a lovely time. They were telling stories to each other about their adventures.

'The other day,' said a large cargo plane called Ferdie, 'I flew to a very hot country, away over the sea, and they loaded me with a lot of cages, full of lions and tigers. They roared, and roared, and kept trying to break out of their cages all the way back.'

'Weren't you frightened?' asked one of the other planes.

'Of course not,' said Ferdie. 'We freighters get used to things like that.'

'The last time I was out,' said one of the airliners, 'I was caught up in a terrible storm. If I hadn't had such good engines, I'd never have reached home.'

'I was in a bad storm once,' said Henry, 'and . . .'

But no one listened to Henry. He was only a helicopter, and they were big planes. They all turned their backs on him, and went on talking and laughing among themselves. Poor Henry! He felt very lonely and unhappy by himself in his corner. He was just wishing and wishing that he could go out, when the hangar door opened, and in came Sam.

'Come along,' he called cheerily. 'It's stopped snowing.'
Sam pushed him out of the hangar.

'Brrr!' shivered Henry, as the wind whistled round his
rotors. 'It *is* cold.'

Beside the hangar was a small red van. When the driver
saw Henry he opened the back doors, and pulled out three
sacks.

'Wait a moment,' said Sam. 'I'll help you load them.'

They lifted the sacks one by one, and put them inside
Henry's cabin. Then Sam started Henry's engine, his rotors
swished, and his wheels came off the ground.

'Good-bye,' shouted the van driver. 'Deliver my letters
and parcels safely. They're Christmas presents and cards for
the children.'

'We will,' shouted Sam.

Henry flew on steadily, looking down on a hushed, white
world. There were no other planes up, and most of the cars
and buses were at home in their garages.

'We're going to a little village up among the mountains,'

explained Sam. 'It has snowed so much, that the postman can't take his load up the road.'

On and on flew Henry. He passed over the big town, but today there were very few people in the streets, and no one looked up when Henry went over. He passed over the river and headed towards the mountains. Sam eased him gently up and up. The higher he got, the colder it was. Poor Henry's rotors were chattering, and even Sam, in his warm flying suit, was beginning to feel very shivery. All at once Henry could see a church steeple in a clump of trees.

'There it is!' cried Sam. 'We've arrived. Well done, Henry.'

They went down and down, until they were hovering just over the village green. Henry could see the children having a wonderful time. Some were building a snow-man, a great fat white one, with pieces of coal for eyes, a pipe in its mouth, and an old battered hat on its head. Other children were sliding on tea trays down the hill by the church, and some other boys and girls were skating on a frozen pond nearby. In one corner of the green a snowball fight was in progress.

But they all stopped what they were doing when they saw Henry.

'It's a helicopter,' they shouted. 'Hurrah!' Then one naughty little boy aimed two snowballs at Henry.

Sam tied a long rope to the top of one of the sacks, and let it down gently. The village postman came running out of his office pushing a wheel-barrow. He loaded the sack on to his barrow, and untied the rope. Sam pulled it up, and tied another sack to the end of the rope. He let that down, and the third sack, too. The postman loaded all the sacks

on to his barrow. Then he waved his cap to Henry and pushed the wheel-barrow into the post-office.

Just as Henry was about to set off for home, the policeman came running up.

'Wait a minute, Henry,' he called. 'Will you do something else for us?'

'Of course,' said Henry cheerily.

'The lorry from the big town is stuck at the bottom of the mountain. He has the chickens for our Christmas dinner, and our Christmas trees. Can you bring them up for us?'

'I'll try,' promised Henry.

Sam took him up again, and back towards the big town they flew. Soon they spotted the lorry, stuck fast in a snowdrift.

'Hello, lorry-driver,' shouted Henry. 'Can I help you?'

The lorry-driver poked his head out of his cabin.

'Why, if it isn't a little helicopter! Can you take my goods up to the village? I'm stuck!'

'That's just what I've come for,' called Henry. 'Sam will let down a rope, and we'll load the boxes into my cabin.'

Henry's cabin was soon stacked high with chickens and Christmas trees, and boxes of Christmas puddings and sweets, so that there was hardly room for Sam to climb back into the driver's seat.

'Good-bye,' shouted Henry to the driver. 'We'll take your load to the village, and then we'll come back and tell them in the big town to send a tractor to pull you out.'

'Good-bye, and thank you,' shouted the lorry-driver.

Back over the village green hovered Henry. The policeman and the postman, and the children and their mothers and fathers cheered and cheered as the goods were unloaded. When the last box was on the ground one of the children tied something to the end of the rope.

'A present for you and Henry,' she called. 'Thank you very much for bringing our dinners and presents. Happy Christmas!'

Sam pulled up the parcel. Inside was a lovely box of sweets, and a tiny Christmas tree, decorated with silver balls and tinsel. The note read: 'The sweets for Sam. The tree for Henry, with love from the children.'

Sam and Henry *were* pleased.

'Thank you very much, children,' they called. 'Happy Christmas!'

Then Henry waggled his rotors, and Sam waved his hat, and they flew away towards home. When they reached the aerodrome, Sam fastened the little Christmas tree on the top of Henry's rotors, pushed him into the hangar, and went off home to tea.

'What have you got there?' asked Ferdie curiously.

'A present from some friends,' said Henry proudly. 'Even helicopters have adventures sometimes.' He looked upwards through his rotor blades. The little tree sparkled and glittered under the hangar lights.

'Well,' said Ferdie rather grudgingly, 'I must admit it does make the hangar look really Christmassy. You must tell us all about it sometime, Henry.'

'Tomorrow,' promised Henry. 'I'm really *too* tired to chatter just now.'

From *Henry the Helicopter*

The Little Wooden Horse

BY URSULA MORAY WILLIAMS

One day Uncle Peder made a little wooden horse. This was not at all an extraordinary thing, for Uncle Peder made toys every day of his life, but oh, this was such a brave little horse, so gay and splendid on his four green wheels, so proud and dashing with his red saddle and blue stripes! Uncle Peder had never made so fine a little horse before.

'I shall ask five shillings for this little wooden horse!' he cried.

What was his surprise when he saw large tears trickling down the newly painted face of the little wooden horse.

'Don't do that!' said Uncle Peder. 'Your paint will run. And what is there to cry about? Do you want more spots on your sides? Do you wish for bigger wheels? Do you creak? Are you stiff? Aren't your stripes broad enough? Upon my word I see nothing to cry about! I shall certainly sell you for five shillings!'

But the tears still ran down the newly painted cheeks of the little wooden horse, till at last Uncle Peder lost patience. He picked him up and threw him on the pile of wooden toys he meant to sell in the morning. The little wooden horse said nothing at all but went on crying. When night came and the toys slept in the sack under Uncle Peder's chair the tears were still running down the cheeks of the little wooden horse.

In the morning Uncle Peder picked up the sack and set out to sell his toys.

At every village he came to the children ran out to meet him, crying, 'Here's Uncle Peder! Here's Uncle Peder come to sell his wooden toys!'

Then out of the cottages came the mothers and the fathers, the grandpas and the grandmas, the uncles and the aunts, the elder cousins and the godparents, to see what Uncle Peder had to sell.

The children who had birthdays were very fortunate: they had the best toys given to them, and could choose what they would like to have. The children who had been good in school were lucky too. Their godparents bought them wooden pencil-boxes and rulers and paper-cutters, like grown-up people. The little ones had puppets, dolls, marionettes, and tops. Uncle Peder had made them all, painting

the dolls in red and yellow, the tops in blue, scarlet, and green. When the children had finished choosing, their mothers, fathers, grandpas, grandmas, uncles, aunts, elder cousins, and godparents sent them home, saying, 'Now let's hear no more of you for another year!' Then they stayed behind to gossip with old Peder, who brought them news from other villages he had passed by on his way.

Nobody bought the little wooden horse, for nobody had five shillings to spend. The fathers and the mothers, the grandpas and the grandmas, the uncles and the aunts, the elder cousins and the godparents, all shook their heads, saying, 'Five shillings! Well, that's too much! Won't you take any less, Uncle Peder?'

But Uncle Peder would not take a penny less.

'You see, I have never made such a fine little horse before,' he said.

All the while the tears ran down the nose of the little wooden horse, who looked very sad indeed, so that when Uncle Peder was alone once more he asked him, 'Tell me, my little wooden horse, what is there to cry about? Have I driven the nails crookedly into your legs? Don't you like your nice green wheels and your bright blue stripes? What is there to cry about, I'd like to know?'

At last the little wooden horse made a great effort and sobbed out, 'Oh, master, I don't want to leave you! I'm a quiet little horse, I don't want to be sold. I want to stay with you for ever and ever. I shouldn't cost much to keep, master. Just a little bit of paint now and then; perhaps a little oil in my wheels once a year. I'll serve you faithfully, master, if only you won't sell me for five shillings. I'm a quiet little horse, I am, and the thought of going out into the wide

world breaks my heart. Let me stay with you here, master –
oh, do!'

Uncle Peder scratched his head as he looked in surprise
at his little wooden horse.

'Well,' he said, 'that's a funny thing to cry about! Most
of my toys want to go out into the wide world. Still, as nobody wants to give five shillings for you, and you have such
a sad expression, you can stop with me for the present, and
maybe I won't get rid of you after all.'

When Uncle Peder said this the little wooden horse
stopped crying at once, and galloped three times round in a
circle.

'Why, you're a gay fellow after all!' said Uncle Peder, as
the little wooden horse kicked his legs in the air, so that the
four green wheels spun round and round.

'Who would have thought it,' said Uncle Peder.

From *Adventures of the Little Wooden Horse*

The Dog and His Tail

There was a little dog, and he had a little tail,
And he used to wag, wag, wag it.
But whenever he was sad, because he had been bad,
On the ground he would drag, drag, drag it.

CLIVE SANSOM

Little Pig Barnaby

BY URSULA HOURIHANE

Little Pig Barnaby lived by himself in a dear little cottage at the edge of a wood. He grew potatoes and cabbages and blue forget-me-nots in his small garden, and sometimes, when he wanted a special treat, he went into the wood and nosed up a few acorns from the ground around the big oak tree. In the winter, when he couldn't grow much in his garden, Little Pig Barnaby took a basket and went off down the lane, along the white high-road, and into the town to buy whatever he wanted to eat.

One day, Little Pig Barnaby had a lovely surprise. His Great Aunt Susannah sent him a shiny sixpence. Little Pig Barnaby was so excited when he opened his Great Aunt Susannah's parcel that he nearly forgot to read the letter inside. He turned the shiny sixpence over and over in his paw and wondered what he should buy with it.

'I could buy some potato seed,' he said to himself. 'But that wouldn't be very exciting, when I have to buy potato seed anyhow.'

He thought a bit more.

'I could buy a big white handkerchief,' he said, 'to put in my pocket when I go to town to do my shopping. But my grandmother generally sends me a white handkerchief for Christmas, so that wouldn't be very exciting either.'

He thought a bit more.

And as he was thinking he suddenly noticed Great Aunt Susannah's letter sticking out of the parcel wrappings.

77

'Goodness me!' he said. 'I nearly forgot to read my letter. I wonder what it says.' And he opened the letter and began to read. This is what Great Aunt Susannah said in her letter:

Dear Barnaby,

When I went in the Park this morning I saw a little boy with a beautiful yellow balloon and I thought, 'What fun! I know Barnaby would like a balloon to play with.' So I am sending you sixpence, specially for a balloon.

Your affectionate
Great Aunt Susannah

'Well!' said Barnaby. 'How exciting! How kind of Great Aunt Susannah to help me to get a balloon.'

And then he began to think a bit more and he found he didn't quite know what a balloon was! But he was sure it was something very nice or Great Aunt Susannah wouldn't have wanted him to have one so specially.

'I'll ask someone as I go to town,' he said to himself. 'Then I shall know which shop to go to.'

He got out his basket, put on his best blue tie, and went out of his little house and locked the door behind him.

It was a sunny, blowy afternoon and Little Pig Barnaby felt very happy and excited as he trotted down the lane to go to town.

Just round the corner, past the big oak tree where he found his acorns sometimes, Little Pig Barnaby met Bobtail the Rabbit.

'Hullo, Bobtail!' he called. 'I am so glad to see you. You know a lot about everything. My Great Aunt Susannah has sent me sixpence to buy a balloon. But I don't think I quite know what a balloon looks like. Can you tell me?'

Bobtail scratched his head with his paw and looked very wise. 'Ah, yes,' he said. 'Of course, of course. A balloon! Let me see. A balloon is round and fat and red. Yes, Little Pig Barnaby, that's what a balloon is. Round and fat and red.'

'Oh, thank you very much,' said Little Pig Barnaby, and he said good-bye to Bobtail the Rabbit and hurried on his way.

'Round and fat and red,' he said to himself as he went. 'And Great Aunt Susannah's little boy had a yellow one. So they must be round and fat and red, *or* round and fat and yellow. Bobtail didn't say where I could buy one. I'd better ask someone else. They might be able to tell me.'

He trotted out of the lane and on to the great white highroad.

Presently he saw a small black dog coming along the road towards him. The little black dog sniffed in the hedgerow and wagged his tail. He looked very friendly and nice. Little Pig Barnaby thought he would ask him about the balloon.

'Excuse me,' he said politely, 'but do you know where I could buy a balloon? They're round and fat and red, you know. And sometimes they're round and fat and yellow.'

The little black dog wagged his tail and said, 'Woof! Woof! Round and fat and red, you said? Or round and fat and yellow? Why don't you ask the greengrocer? He sells apples, and they're round and fat and red. And oranges. And they're round and fat and yellow. I should try at the greengrocer's, Little Pig, if I were you.'

'Oh, thank you,' said Little Pig Barnaby happily. 'That is a very good idea. I will.' And he went along the great white high-road whistling a little tune to himself because he felt so excited and pleased.

Presently he came to the beginning of the town and he began to look to left and to right to see if he could find a greengrocer's shop where he could buy his balloon. Very soon he found one. He clutched his shiny sixpence and opened the door. There was a nice old lady inside the greengrocer's shop. She looked at Little Pig Barnaby and smiled. 'And what can I do for you, my dear?' she asked kindly.

Little Pig Barnaby held out his shiny sixpence and said, 'Please, could I buy a balloon? A red one or a yellow one.'

The old lady shook her head. 'I'm sorry, my dear,' she said. 'We don't sell balloons here. You've come to the wrong shop, I'm afraid.'

'Oh dear,' said Little Pig Barnaby sadly. 'I did hope you would have balloons. You have round fat red apples and round fat yellow oranges, haven't you? I thought you might have round fat red and yellow balloons too.'

'No, my dear,' said the old lady. 'You'll have to go to Miss Simpkins' shop down the street. She has lots of lovely toys there and I'm sure she'll be able to sell you just the kind of balloon you want.'

Little Pig Barnaby thanked the old lady and went off down the street again. Presently, he came to a beautiful shop painted green and white and the window was simply *full* of toys.

'Ooh!' said Little Pig Barnaby excitedly. 'This must be Miss Simpkins' toyshop.' He opened the door and went in. A little bell went PING! as the door opened, and Miss Simpkins came hurrying in from somewhere at the back of the shop. She smiled at Little Pig Barnaby and said, 'And what can I get for you, my dear?'

Little Pig Barnaby held out his shiny sixpence and said, 'Please, could I buy a balloon?'

'Why, certainly, my dear!' said Miss Simpkins. 'Here they are. Which colour would you like best? I've red balloons, blue balloons, yellow balloons, and green balloons.' And she showed him a box of funny-shaped rubber things that didn't look a bit like balloons. Little Pig Barnaby didn't know what to say. He was so disappointed. He just looked and looked.

'Don't you like them?' Miss Simpkins asked in great surprise.

'I'm sure they're very nice,' said Little Pig Barnaby politely, 'but I thought balloons were round and fat.'

'Oh dear, dear!' laughed Miss Simpkins. 'Of course balloons are round and fat when they are blown up. Just you watch,' and she picked up a small blue shape and began to blow into it – Poo-of! Poo-of! Little Pig Barnaby stared and stared. The balloon grew fatter and fatter and rounder and rounder. Poo-of! Poo-of! blew Miss Simpkins, and rounder and rounder and fatter and fatter grew the blue balloon.

'There!' cried Miss Simpkins at last. 'Isn't that a nice round fat balloon for you?'

'Oh YES!' cried Little Pig Barnaby. 'Thank you, thank you! That's the loveliest balloon in the world. May I have it for my shiny sixpence?'

'Of course you may,' said Miss Simpkins, and she tied up the balloon tightly, leaving a nice long end for Little Pig Barnaby to hold.

And Little Pig Barnaby said 'Thank you' all over again and hurried away home with his beautiful blue balloon, as round and fat as could be.

'I'm the happiest little pig in the world,' he said. 'And I like round fat BLUE balloons best in the world. Hurrah! Hurrah!'

From *Little Pig Barnaby and Other Stories*

The Surprise Christmas Tree

BY URSULA HOURIHANE

There was once a little old man who lived all by himself in a cottage at the edge of a wood. He was rather a lonely old man, but he had lots of friends among the birds of the wood and the hedgerow. They all loved the little old man because he was always kind to them. If any small bird hurt its wing or leg, the little old man would always bandage it up. And if it was cold and the snow lay thick on the ground so that there was no food for the birds, the little old man always shared his dinner with them or threw out his crumbs and crusts for the hungry birds to eat.

One day, just before Christmas, the little old man was feeling rather sad.

'If only I had someone to share my Christmas fun,' he said. 'I should so like to have a Christmas Tree. But that would be silly for an old man like me, living all alone.'

And then, quite suddenly, the little old man had an idea. A really splendid idea.

He got up from his armchair by the fire, put on his big Wellington boots and his bright red muffler and his battered old hat, fetched a spade from his back kitchen, and set off for the woods.

When the little old man came home again at tea-time he was carrying a lovely little fir tree under his arm. He brought it into the cottage and shut the door tightly. Then he fetched a big red flower-pot full of earth. He planted the little fir tree in the big red flower-pot and put it in his front room. Then he drew the curtains tight across the window so that no one could see in.

'I don't want anyone to guess my secret,' he said.

Presently Robin Redbreast came along. He looked at the window and saw the curtains drawn tightly across.

'Cheep-cheep,' said Robin Redbreast. 'What's in there? Why has the little old man drawn his curtains so early?'

Tommy Thrush went flying by.

'Cheep-cheep,' said Tommy Thrush. 'What's in there? Why has the little old man drawn his curtains so early?'

Billy Bluetit fluttered down. He pecked at the window, tap, tap, tap!

'Cheep-cheep,' said Billy Bluetit. 'What's in there? Why has the little old man drawn his curtains so early?'

Sammy Starling fluttered to the window-sill.

'Cheep-cheep,' he squawked. 'What's in there? Why has the little old man drawn his curtains so early?'

All the birds were very puzzled.

But the little old man wouldn't draw his curtains back.

At last, it was Christmas Day. The little old man woke up quite early. He hurried downstairs and opened his front door. The soft white snow was sparkling in the sunshine and the sky was clear and blue.

'Happy Christmas!' the little old man called to all his bird friends.

'Happy Christmas!' they all sang back to him.

Then the little old man went back into his cottage again.

'He's gone to find some crumbs for our breakfast,' said the birds. 'How kind he is!'

But the little old man didn't come back with any crumbs for the birds' breakfast. What do you think he had gone to

Then our mother said, 'That child must have a bed!' Even though our father managed to mend the cot, our mother said, 'She must have a bed!'

My naughty little sister said, 'A big bed for me?'

And our mother said, 'I am afraid so, you bad child. You are too rough now for your poor old cot.'

My little sister wasn't ashamed of being too rough for her cot. She was pleased because she was going to have the new bed, and she said, 'A big girl's bed for me!'

My little sister told everybody that she was going to have a big girl's bed. She told her kind friend the window-cleaner man, and the coalman, and the milkman. She told the dustman too. She said, 'You can have my old cot soon, dustman, because I am going to have a big girl's bed.' And she was as pleased as pleased.

But our mother wasn't pleased at all. She was rather worried. You see our mother was afraid that my naughty little sister would jump and jump on her new bed, and scratch it, and treat it badly. My naughty little sister had done such dreadful things to her old cot, that my mother was afraid she would spoil her new bed too.

Well now, my little sister told the lady who lived next door all about her new bed. The lady who lived next door to us was called Mrs Jones, but my little sister used to call her Mrs Cocoa Jones because she used to go in and have a cup of cocoa with her every morning.

Mrs Cocoa Jones was a very kind lady, and when she heard about the new bed she said, 'I have a little yellow eiderdown and a yellow counterpane upstairs, and they are too small for any of my beds, so when your new bed comes I will give them to you.'

My little sister was excited, but when she told our mother what Mrs Cocoa had said, our mother shook her head.

'Oh dear,' she said, 'WHAT will happen to the lovely eiderdown and counterpane when our bad little girl has them?'

Then, a kind aunt who lived near us said, 'I have a dear little green nightie-case put away in a drawer. It belonged to me when I was a little girl. When your new bed comes you can have it to put your nighties in like a big girl.'

My little sister said, 'Good. Good,' because of all the nice things she was going to have for her bed. But our mother was more worried than ever. She said, 'Oh dear! That *pretty* nightie-case. You'll spoil it, I know you will!'

But my little sister went on being pleased as pleased about it.

Then one day the new bed arrived. It was a lovely shiny brown bed, new as new, with a lovely blue stripy mattress to go on it: new as new. And there was a new stripy pillow too. Just like a real big girl would have.

My little sister watched while my mother took the poor old cot to pieces, and stood it up against the wall. She watched when the new bed was put up, and the new mattress was laid on top of it. She watched the new pillow being put into a clean white case, and when our mother made the bed with clean new sheets and clean new blankets. She said, 'Really big-girl! A big girl's bed – all for me.'

Then Mrs Cocoa Jones came in, and she was carrying the pretty yellow eiderdown and the yellow counterpane. They were very shiny and satiny like buttercup flowers, and when our mother put them on top of the new bed, they looked BEAUTIFUL.

Then our kind aunt came down the road, and *she* was carrying a little parcel, and in the little parcel was the pretty green nightie-case. My little sister ran down the road to meet her because she was so excited. She was more excited still when our aunt picked up her little nightdress and put it into the pretty green case and laid the green case on the yellow shiny eiderdown.

My little sister was so pleased that she was GLAD WHEN BEDTIME CAME.

And what do you think? She got carefully into bed with Rosy-primrose, and she laid herself down and stretched herself out – carefully, carefully, like a good, nice girl.

And she didn't jump and jump, and she didn't scratch the shiny brown wood, or scribble with pencils or scrape with tin-lids. Not ever! Not even when she had had the new bed for a long long time.

My little sister took great care of her big girl's bed. She took great care of her shiny yellow eiderdown and counterpane and her pretty green nightie-case.

And whatever do you think she said to me?

She said, 'You had the fairy pink cot before I did. But this is my VERY OWN BIG GIRL'S BED, and I am going to take great care of my very own bed, like a big girl!'

From *More Naughty Little Sister Stories*

I had a little hen,
The prettiest ever seen;
She washed up the dishes,
And kept the house clean.
She went to the mill
To fetch me some flour,
And always got home
In less than an hour.
She baked me my bread,
She brewed me my ale,
She sat by the fire
And told a fine tale.

NURSERY RHYME

The Three Little Pigs

TRADITIONAL

Once upon a time there were three little pigs. One day the first little pig set out to find a home for himself.

On the way he met a man carrying a bundle of straw. 'Please will you give me some of your straw so that I can build a house?' asked the first little pig.

'Of course I will,' said the man, and he gave the little pig his bundle of straw. Soon the first little pig built his house and very nice it was – but not very strong.

By and by the big Wolf came along and walked all round the house. 'Ho, ho, little pig, may I come in?' he called through the keyhole.

'No, no, by the hair of my chinny-chin-chin,' said the little pig.

'Then I'll huff and I'll puff and I'll blow your house in!' The Wolf huffed and he puffed and he blew the house in, so the first little pig had to run away and hide in the wood.

Next day the second little pig set out to find a home for himself. On the way he met a man carrying a bundle of sticks.

'Please will you give me some of your sticks so that I can build a house?' asked the second little pig.

'Of course I will,' said the man and he gave the little pig his sticks. The little pig built his house and very nice it was – but not very strong.

By and by the big Wolf came along and walked all round the house. 'Ho, ho, little pig, may I come in?' he called through the keyhole.

'No, no, by the hair of my chinny-chin-chin.'

'Then I'll huff and I'll puff and I'll blow your house in!'
The Wolf huffed and he puffed and he blew the house in, so
the second little pig had to run away and hide in the wood.

Next day the third little pig set out to find a home for
himself. On the way he met a man with a load of bricks.
'Please will you give me some bricks so that I can build a
house?' asked the third little pig.

'Of course I will,' said the man and gave the little pig his
bricks. Soon the third little pig built his house and very nice
it was – and very strong too.

By and by the big Wolf came along and walked all round
the house. 'Ho, ho, little pig, may I come in?' he called
through the keyhole.

'No, no, by the hair of my chinny-chin-chin.'

'Then I'll huff and I'll puff and I'll blow your house in.'

He huffed and he puffed and he puffed and he huffed, but
he could not blow the house in. So he tried again. He huffed
and he puffed and he huffed; and he puffed and he huffed
and he puffed, but he could *not* blow the house in.

'Then I'll come down the chimney!' shouted the Wolf in a rage.

'Do!' said the third little pig, laughing to himself, and he put a big pan of water on the fire.

Then the bad Wolf did come down the chimney, and splash, he fell right into the pan of water. And that was the end of him!

So the third little pig and the second little pig and the first little pig all lived together in the little brick house. And very happy they were.

The Little Red Engine Goes to Market

BY DIANA ROSS

It was Tuesday, and the Little Red Engine was glad. For Tuesday was market day, and how the Little Red Engine loved market day! For on market days it had four extra vans and an extra carriage and a truck as well, and then how proud it felt, and strong and important.

'WHOOEEE,' it whistled as it ran from its shed. 'It's market day today and we mustn't be late.'

And it could hardly wait for its drink of water from the big hydrant by the signal box.

And as soon as it had finished, 'WHOOEEE. I'm coming, I'm coming.'

And away it went chuffa, chuffa, chuffa, chuff. Chuffa, chuffa, chuffa, chuff.

Usually it sang dig-a-dig dig, dig-a-dig dig. But with all the extra load behind its song grew more important, and so it should!

CHUFFA CHUFFA CHUFFA CHUFF. CHUFFA CHUFFA CHUFFA CHUFF. CHUFFA CHUFFA CHUFF.

The first halt it came to was Dodge. And as it got near, 'WHOOEE. WHOOEE. I'm going to market. Who is coming with me?'

And it slowed up at the platform SHUHHHHHH.

The porter cried, 'There's a crate of hens from old Mrs Ransome.'

And the hens all cried, 'Cluck, cluck, cluck, cluck. Cluck cluck cluck cluck.'

And the cock among them cried, 'Cock-a-doodle-doo', just to show who was master.

'We are going to market and we mustn't be late.'

'Well, in you get and away we go. WHOOOOEEEE.'

And on they went with a chuffa, chuffa, chuffa, chuff.

Then they came to Mazy, and as they got near, 'WHOOOEEE. I am going to market. Who is coming with me?'

And it slowed up at the platform SHUUUHHHHHHH.

The porter cried, 'There's a crate of ducks and geese from Farmer Gregory's yard.'

And the ducks cried, 'Quack Quack Quack.'

And the geese poked their long necks between the bars of the crate, 'Hisssss. Hissssss. We are going to market, and we mustn't be late.'

'In you get and away we go. WHOOOEEEE.'

And on they went, chuffa chuffa chuffa chuff.

Next came Callington Humble. As they got near, 'WHOOOEEE. I am going to market. Who is coming with me?'

And it drew up at the platform SHUUUH.

The porter cried, 'There's three of the Baronet's prize flock of Jerseys.'

And the Jersey cows cried, 'MOOOOO, MOOOO, MOOOOOO,' in their soft voices. 'We are going to market. We mustn't be late.'

'In you get and away we go. WHOOOEEE.' And on they went, chuffa chuffa chuffa chuff.

And then they came to Never Over.

'WHOOOEEE. I am going to market. Who is coming with me?'

The porter cried, 'There's the gamekeeper's cat going to the vet.'

And the cat said, 'Miaow, Miaow. I was hunting last night and I broke my front paw in a trap.'

And the Little Red Engine cried, 'WHOOOEEE. How it must have hurt you. Don't cry, Pussy. The vet will make it better. In you get and away we go. WHOOOEEE.'

And on they went with a chuffa chuffa chuffa chuff.

But when they came to Merrymans Rising, with all the extra load behind the Little Red Engine panted and puffed. HUTCHA BA HUTCHA BA HUTCHA BA BAAAA, until it reached the top and then it ran down to Soke the other side.

'WHOOOEEE WHOOOOEEEE.'

And it drew up at the platform quite out of breath SHHHHHHHHHHHHH.

'I'm going to market. Who is coming with me?'

The porter cried, 'There's a flock of Southdown lambs.'

And the lambs all cried, 'Baaa Baaaa Baaaa.'

And Trusty the sheep-dog cried, 'WOOOF WOOOF. Hurry along there. You mustn't keep them waiting. You're going to market. You mustn't be late.'

'In you get and away we go. WHOOOEEEE.'

And on they went, chuffa chuffa chuffa chuff.

At Seven Sisters two colts from Noman's stables were prancing about the platform.

As the Little Red Engine came in, SHUUHHHHHHH.

'HEEEEE, HEEEEEE,' cried the colts. 'We thought you were never coming. We are going to market and mustn't be late.'

'In you get and away we go. WHOOOOEEEE.'

But the colts kicked up their heels and wouldn't get in and shied and reared for all they had been so impatient.

'Get along in or I'll certainly go without you. WHOOOOOEEEE.'

And then they got in, and away they went, chuffa chuffa chuffa chuff.

And at last they all came to Dumble. As they got near,

'WHOOOEEE. I'm going to market. Who is coming with me?'

And it slowed up at the platform, SHUHHHHHH.

The porter cried, 'There's a new yellow tractor from the Dumble Agricultural Depot.'

And the tractor went, 'UUUR UUUR UUUR. I'm going to market and mustn't be late.'

'In you get and away we go. WHOOOOEEEEE.'

And as they got near Taddlecombe, 'WHOOOOOOOOO,' whistled the Little Red Engine. 'We are just coming in. Everyone get ready. The market is beginning. We are only just in time.'

And they drew into the platform, SHUHHHHHHHHHH.

And first came out the tractor, and then came out the colts, and then came out the sheep, and then hopped out the gamekeeper's cat, and then came out the cows, and then came out the geese and ducks, and then came out the cock and hens, and they all cried out, 'Good-bye, Good-bye, and thank you for the journey.'

And the Little Red Engine replied, 'WHOOOOOEEE. Good-bye, Good-bye. Good luck in the market.'

And away it ran to its shed.

'How I do love market day. SHUHHHHHHH.'

From *The Little Red Engine Goes to Market*

Oliver and the Scarecrow

BY GWENDA M. ALLEN

Oliver woke up early and looked through the window. In the paddock across the road Mr Pym, the scarecrow, stood very straight and stiff in the sunlight. Round the feet the cabbage leaves sparkled as though they had been polished. There was one ball of fluff in the sky.

Oliver went to the kitchen.

'I think I had better wear my new raincoat and sou'wester today,' he said.

Oliver's mother looked through the doorway. The sky was very blue. She laughed.

'There is a cloud over Mr Pym's paddock,' said Oliver quickly.

'Very well,' said his mother, and she took the shining new raincoat out of the cupboard.

As he passed Mr Pym's paddock Oliver said, 'Good morning.'

'Good morning,' said Mr Pym. 'You won't get wet to-day.'

'No,' said Oliver.

He looked at the small cloud; it seemed a little larger. But as he walked along in his new raincoat, Oliver felt hotter and hotter.

At lunch-time the sun went in, pulling the grey clouds round itself.

At three o'clock the rain came. Oliver splashed home from school in his shining new raincoat. Drops of water

99

from his sou'wester fell on to his shoulders and slid quickly to the ground.

'I am as dry as an almond in its shell,' said Oliver. 'I am as dry as a rabbit in his burrow.'

And the drops of rain fell on his shoulders and slid to the ground.

When he came to Mr Pym's paddock Oliver said, 'Good afternoon.'

The scarecrow said nothing. His old brown coat was soaked with rain. Streams of water poured from the brim of his hat. Drops of water trickled down his cheeks; they looked like tears.

'What is the matter?' asked Oliver. 'Are you wet?'

'Take a look at me,' replied Mr Pym. 'Of course I'm wet.'

'I meant, don't you like being wet?' asked Oliver.

'Does anybody?' moaned Mr Pym. 'Do you?'

'No,' said Oliver. 'No, I don't.'

Two drops of water splashed down the scarecrow's face.

'You can run out of the rain,' he said, 'but here am I, fixed in one place. It is all very nice to be a scarecrow when the sun is out. But I would rather be you when it rains.'

Oliver took off his shining new raincoat. He put it on Mr Pym. A scarecrow's arms are very stiff. It was hard to put his arms through the sleeves.

'Now you will be as dry as an almond in its shell,' said Oliver. 'You will be as dry as a rabbit in his burrow.'

'As soon as the rain stops you may have your raincoat back,' said Mr Pym.

'Thank you,' said Oliver.

When Oliver got home he was very wet.

'Silly child!' cried his mother. 'You will wear your raincoat when the sun is out, and you take it off when it rains.'

Oliver looked through the window. The sun was coming out again. It shone on the cabbages in Mr Pym's paddock. It shone on Oliver's new raincoat. Oliver guessed that the scarecrow was smiling.

'How wet you are!' said Oliver's mother. 'You look like a scarecrow.'

Oliver smiled to himself.

'And the scarecrow looks like me,' he said.

But he didn't say it very loudly.

From *Oliver*

Kindness to Animals

Riddle cum diddle cum dido,
My little dog's name is Fido;
  I bought him a wagon,
  And hitched up a dragon,
And off we both went for a ride, oh!

Riddle cum diddle cum doodle,
My little cat's name is Toodle;
  I curled up her hair,
  But she only said, 'There!
You have made me look *just* like a poodle!'

Riddle cum diddle cum dinky,
My little pig's name is Winky;
  I keep him quite clean
  With the washing machine,
And I rinse him all off in the sinkie.

LAURA RICHARDS

Benjamin Bear, Stationmaster

BY URSULA HOURIHANE

Benjamin Bear was just going to help himself to honey when he heard a loud rat-tat at the front door.

'Postman sounds very important this morning,' he said to his wife Tabitha. 'I'd better hurry and see what it's all about.'

He put back the honey spoon and went to the door. The postman was holding a large official-looking envelope in his hand.

'Something interesting for you today, Benjamin,' he said. 'I hope it's good news.'

'My word, yes!' said Benjamin. 'What a lot of grand seals it has. And look at the gold crown marked on the back! What *can* it be?'

'Must be from the King, I should think,' said the postman excitedly. 'I can't stop now, but you will let me know if it's anything extra special, won't you, Benjamin?'

'Of course I will,' said Benjamin Bear, and he hurried back to Tabitha. 'Just look at this envelope,' he said. 'It must be something very important. Postman thinks it might be from the King! Do you think so, Tabitha?'

'Why not open it and find out?' said his wife. 'And don't forget in your excitement, my dear, that the nine o'clock train is due in twenty minutes and you've still got your bedroom slippers on.'

Benjamin Bear, who was the Stationmaster at Half-way Halt, looked at the clock hastily. It was true. There were only twenty minutes to spare before he had to be on the platform with his red and green flags and his shining silver whistle, all ready for work.

He opened the grand envelope as fast as his paws would let him and drew out a large sheet of thick white paper. He smoothed it out carefully, propped it against the toast rack, and began to read.

Dear Sir,

This is to notify you that His Majesty the King will be passing through your station on Wednesday next at three o'clock.

Please see that all is in order and looking as nice as possible.

Kindly keep the line clear.

The Royal Train will hoot three times to let you know it's coming.

Yours truly,

The King's Secretary.

P.S. You may wave both your flags together as it's a Special Occasion.

P.P.S. I enclose sixpence so that you can buy a bit of extra polish for your buttons and things. His Majesty is very particular about polishing.

'Well!' cried Benjamin Bear excitedly. 'Whoever would have thought the King's train would pass through my station?'

'What an honour! and what a Special Occasion! Why! it's Tuesday today, Tabitha! The King will be coming to-morrow. Good gracious! we must get busy at once.'

'Where's the sixpence the gentleman said he was sending?' asked Tabitha. 'If you give it to me I'll pop down to the village for some extra polish. Though no one can say your buttons are ever anything but shiny, Benjamin.'

Benjamin Bear poked about in the big envelope and finally pulled out a shining silver sixpence.

'Here you are, my love,' he said. 'Get the best polish you can and we'll dazzle everyone with our beautiful station.'

'Never mind the beautiful station now, Benjamin,' said Tabitha. 'The nine o'clock will be here in a minute and you should be on the platform. Here, take your cap and flags and run.' And she bundled Benjamin into his uniform jacket and out of the door. Benjamin hurried down the garden path and through the gate to the station platform just in time to hear the nine o'clock whistling under the bridge.

'Morning, Benjamin!' called the Engine Driver cheerfully, as he slowed down and brought the train to a stop.

'Good morning!' cried Benjamin. 'I hope you've had a good run?'

'Splendid, thank you,' said the Engine Driver. Then he laughed. 'Did you oversleep this morning, Stationmaster?'

Benjamin looked surprised. 'No, of course not,' he said. 'But I've had a bit of a scramble to get on the platform before you arrived. I had the most exciting letter, Engine Driver, to say the King is coming in the Royal Train tomorrow afternoon. Isn't that wonderful? I was so excited I nearly forgot the time.'

'My, my!' cried the Engine Driver. 'I should think so indeed. You'll be busy today, Benjamin. Well, it's time I was off. Good luck to you, and don't forget to change your slippers when the King comes tomorrow!'

Benjamin Bear looked at his feet. He was still wearing his blue check slippers!

'My goodness!' he cried as he waved his green flag, 'what a thing to do!' He blew his silver whistle and the train began to puff slowly out of the station. 'I must dash straight home and put on my proper shoes. Tabitha *will* be upset,' he said.

What a busy day that was for Benjamin and Tabitha! They scrubbed and polished and swept and dusted the little station till it was as clean as a new pin. Everyone in the village helped as best they could. The Squire sent down four green tubs with pink geraniums to decorate the platform. The schoolchildren made gaily coloured paperchains to hand from pillar to pillar. Old Mrs Postlethwaite from the Post Office lent her big flag that was only used on high days and holidays. Certainly Benjamin's station did look a picture. By half past two on Wednesday there was hardly a square inch of room on the long platform.

'We'll have the children in front,' said Benjamin, 'Then they can wave their flags and cheer better.'

The Squire stood beside one of his tubs, and Tabitha, Mrs Postlethwaite, and the schoolmistress each stood by one of the others. At the back of the platform, standing rather shakily on a large luggage trolley, was the Village Band. There was Mr Puffin, the trumpet player; Bert Banger, who played the drum; and Miss Popham with her flute. Benjamin himself stood on a small square of red carpet that led out from the Ticket Office to the edge of the platform. He held his green flag in his right paw and the red one in his left. His buttons twinkled and shone like stars.

'When do you think we'd better begin playing?' Mr Puffin whispered to Benjamin who was inspecting everyone.

'As soon as we hear the three hoots, I should think,' said

Benjamin. 'Then you'll be going well by the time the train actually reaches the platform.'

'I hope His Majesty hears us through all the shouting and cheering,' said Miss Popham fussily. She practised a few twiddly notes on her flute.

'Don't waste your breath now,' Mr Puffin warned her severely. 'It would be a terrible thing if you couldn't blow when the train does come.'

'Hold the flag up well, Billy,' Benjamin called to Mrs Postlethwaite's grandson who had the honour of waving the flag while the Royal Train passed.

Suddenly, in the distance, they heard three shrill hoots.

'It's coming!' cried Benjamin. 'Attention, everyone!' Slowly the Royal Train in all its splendour puffed towards the little station.

'Hurrah! Hurrah!' shouted all the children, waving their flags as they cheered.

Toot! Toot! Toot! went the band. The flag fluttered, the Squire saluted, everyone clapped and shouted, while Benjamin waved his two flags furiously.

And there was the King, leaning out of his carriage window, his golden crown with its sparkling jewels twinkling

in the sunshine, and a broad smile on his round rosy face.

And then, suddenly, and long before the carriage had passed through the station, the King disappeared! A gasp of dismay ran through the cheering crowds. Didn't His Majesty like their grand welcome? Poor Benjamin felt ready to cry. His two flags drooped forlornly and even his shining buttons seemed to lose some of their sparkle. The King hadn't liked his beautiful station enough to bother to go on looking at it while the Royal Train passed through. It was a terrible disappointment.

Then, when the last coach was almost out of sight, an extraordinary thing happened. The Royal Train stopped! And a second later, before their astonished eyes, the train began to shunt slowly back into the station! Everyone stared and stared. As for Benjamin, he didn't know what to think. The next thing he knew was that the King's carriage had come to a standstill right in front of the red carpet where Benjamin was standing. And His Majesty was leaning out of the window beaming delightedly and calling, 'Bravo, Stationmaster! Bravo! This is quite the nicest station I've ever seen. I just had to tell the engine driver to bring me back to have another look, and to thank you and all these good people here for such a splendid welcome.'

Benjamin bowed low. He was quite overcome. Everyone cheered and clapped and waved again.

'And now I fear I must go on,' said the King. 'But before I leave I should like to make you a little present, to remind you of this happy occasion.'

Benjamin bowed low again and took the little packet the King held out to him.

'Wear these on your best uniform,' said the King, 'and

may they shine as brightly as those you're wearing now.'

Benjamin stammered out his grateful thanks. The King saluted. The engine let out a shrill whistle, and, amid renewed cheers, the Royal Train drew slowly out of the station.

'What a wonderful occasion!' cried the Squire coming over to shake hands with Benjamin. 'May we see the King's present?'

Benjamin opened the parcel and inside was a smart leather case. And inside the smart leather case, on a bed of creamy white velvet, lay six shining gold buttons, each with a crown engraved in the centre.

'Oh!' cried Benjamin, quite breathless with delight. And 'Oh!' cried all the people when he held them up for everyone to see.

And to this very day, whenever he wears his best uniform, Benjamin Bear proudly displays down his front the six gold buttons the King gave him. Be sure to look out for them if you should ever pass through Half-way Halt on a Special Occasion!

From *Country Bunch*

Feeding the Ducks

BY MARGARET LAW

Every Sunday afternoon John goes with Daddy to the park to feed the three ducks who live there. John takes a paper bag with him, and inside it he puts a piece of white bread, a piece of brown bread, and a slice of sponge cake.

When they come to the pond, the ducks toddle up from the water one behind the other, wiggle-woggle, wiggle-woggle, wiggle-woggle as fast as they can. Then they stand in a line and say 'Quack! quack! quack!'

John opens the bag. He takes out the white bread and throws it to the big white duck who gobbles it all up. He takes out the brown bread and throws it to the fat brown duck who gobbles it all up. He takes out the sponge cake and throws it to the little baby duck and he too gobbles up every crumb.

'Quack! quack! quack!' they say as if they were asking for more, and they don't stop till Daddy shows them the empty bag. Then they turn round and go wiggle-woggle, wiggle-woggle, wiggle-woggle back to the pond, and Daddy and John walk home to tea.

From *Stories to Tell to the Nursery*

The Snow-man

BY H. L. GEE

'Daddy! Mummy! Look! It's been snowing!'

It was Johnny who was shouting so excitedly while sitting up in bed one winter morning. He had looked out of the window, and what he had seen had made him want to sing.

Snow was on the window-sill. Snow was in the garden – thick snow, white and glistening in the frosty air. Snow was on the branches of the trees and bushes. Snow lay two inches thick on the dustbin lid. Snow was on the garden wall, and on the roofs of the houses. There was snow everywhere; and after Johnny had jumped out of bed and rubbed the frost off the window-pane, he saw a little robin with a red waistcoat hopping about in the snow, and chirping as if asking for crumbs.

Johnny ran into the bedroom where Mummy and Daddy were sleeping, and called, 'Wake up, wake up! Daddy! Mummy! Look! It's been snowing! And it's ever so deep. May I have my sledge and give Gay a ride? May I shovel snow from the path? Please may we make a snow-man, Daddy?'

'Snow!' shouted Gay, who was as excited as Johnny.

After breakfast, Johnny put on his thick overcoat, his woollen helmet, his wellingtons, and his gloves. Mummy gave him a shovel. When he opened the back door he found a heap of snow that had drifted across the path during the night. He began shovelling at once. The snow was clean and dry and beautifully cold, and he had a fine time shovelling. Gay followed him, waving her wooden spade, but she kept sitting in the snow. Once she sat down on Spot, and that made him bark ever so loudly. Soon Gay's little nose was red, and her fingers and toes were so cold that she had to go indoors, but Johnny kept on shovelling snow. He worked so hard while making a path to the gate that he was as warm as toast.

What fun it was tramping in the snow and making deep foot-prints! He couldn't walk quickly because the snow stuck to his wellingtons, and made them very heavy; but it was jolly trudging through the drifts, and pretending he was on his way to the North Pole.

Mummy gave Johnny some crumbs. A minute after he had scattered them over the snow, lots and lots of hungry birds came fluttering down, and among them was the little robin, who kept on chirping as if he were saying, 'Thank you very much, Johnny; thank you very much.'

Presently Daddy got the sledge out, and pulled Johnny and Gay over the snow. They went up a little hill, and then Daddy gave the sledge a big push, and away it went down the hill, faster and faster, swaying this way and that, gliding over the snow so quickly that the houses seemed to fly past. At the foot of the hill the sledge went bump into a great heap of snow, and Johnny fell off, and found himself upside down. Gay rolled over and over; and both shouted, 'Daddy, may we do it again?'

Then they did it again.

Then they did it a third time.

Then they did it a fourth time.

It was lovely!

Then Johnny pulled Gay and Spot on the sledge, but Gay fell off, and Spot would keep jumping about and barking loudly. When Gay began eating snow she had to go indoors once more.

Presently Daddy and Johnny went home for a hot drink. While they were sitting near the fire, warming their hands and toes, they agreed that they liked snow better than anything.

'Daddy,' said Johnny, 'may we make a snow-man in the back garden?'

'I think we can try,' said Daddy.

'And may I go and ask Andrea to come and help?' Johnny begged.

'Of course,' said Mummy.

So Johnny put his wellingtons on again, and his woollen gloves, and his helmet and his coat, and away he went tramping through the snow, and across the road, and up the path to Andrea's house. He knocked at the door. When Andrea's mummy opened it, he said, 'Please may Andrea come and make a snow-man in our garden?'

But Andrea's mummy shook her head. 'I'm sorry, Johnny,' she said. 'Andrea has a cold, and she was coughing all night. I daren't allow her to come out. She has a fire in her bedroom, and she will have to stay there all day. She did want to play in the snow, and she's so disappointed to have to stay indoors.'

'Oh,' said Johnny. 'I am sorry.'

Then he turned back, and went tramping home.

'Andrea's poorly,' he told his mummy and daddy sadly. 'She can't come out today, so we'll have to make our snow-man without her.'

'Come along,' said Daddy. 'We'll make a snow-man this very minute.'

But Johnny did not stir. He was thinking. 'I do wish Andrea could have helped,' he said. 'She would have enjoyed it.'

'Yes,' said Mummy, 'she would.'

'It is a pity,' Daddy agreed.

Suddenly Johnny looked up, smiling. 'I know,' he said brightly. 'We'll make a snow-man, Daddy, but we won't make him in our garden. We'll make him in Andrea's garden, and she'll be able to watch us from the window!'

'That's a very good idea,' said Daddy.

'It's a lovely idea,' said Mummy, kissing Johnny on the end of his little, cold nose.

Off they went. Johnny carried a shovel. Mr Brown took a spade. Gay and Spot went with them. It took them a long time to reach Andrea's garden because Gay kept sitting in the snow, but at last they were there, and Johnny called, 'Andrea! Andrea! We're going to make a snow-man for you!'

Andrea ran to the window, knelt on a chair, and watched. She kept smiling at Johnny, and waving to him. She was so happy.

Well, they worked very hard. Mr Brown dug the snow with his spade. Johnny helped with his shovel. Gay threw snow over Spot, who kept barking all the time. Soon they had a big heap of snow. The patted it all round, and shaped it till it began to look like the body of a snow-man. And what do you think happened while they were busy? Why, the little robin flew into Andrea's garden, perched on the wall, and sang to them! He seemed as pleased as anybody about the snow-man.

Then Mr Brown made a snowball – only a little one. But he began rolling it in the snow, and the more he rolled it – with Johnny's help – the bigger it grew. Soon it was bigger than a football. Mr Brown picked up the huge snowball and put it on top of the heap of snow. The snowball was to be the snow-man's head, of course, but as soon as it was on the pile of snow, Gay picked up Johnny's shovel and

knocked it down. Mr Brown quickly made another snow-ball, and then with his pocket-knife made holes for eyes, and a deep slit for a mouth. Next, he took a bit of snow in his hands, and shaped a nose, and stuck it on the face. After that he went into Andrea's coalhouse, and found two little pieces of coal, and put them in the hollows he had shaped for eyes. Then he felt in his pocket, and brought out an old pipe, and pushed it into the snow-man's mouth. When Johnny saw that, he laughed so much that he had to sit in the snow; and when Andrea saw it from the window, she laughed, too.

As soon as the snow-man was finished, Andrea's mother told them all to go indoors. She gave each of them a cup of hot cocoa and a bun, and though they had already had some lunch, they had worked so hard in the frosty air that they were quite ready for something else to eat and drink. Gay crumbled her bun into little bits, but it did not matter; they opened the window and threw the crumbs to the birds.

As they were looking out of the window they saw something they had never expected, for there was the little robin again. First he perched on the wall. Then he flew on the snow-man's head. Then he hopped on the snow-man's pipe, and while there he sang as merrily as could be.

That made Johnny laugh, and as he laughed he heard somebody else laughing upstairs.

It was Andrea.

From *Johnny Brown*

Going Travelling

Early in the morning as the day is dawning,
See the little puff-puffs, all in a row.
Man on the engine turns a little handle,
Puff, puff, puff and away we go.

ANONYMOUS

The Three Billy-Goats Gruff

TRADITIONAL

Once upon a time there were three billy-goats. The smallest was called Gruff, the middle-sized one was called Gruff, and the biggest was called Gruff.

One day the billy-goats set out for a hill where there was good grass to eat. At the bottom of the hill was a river and over the river was a bridge and under the bridge was a great ugly Troll. His eyes were as big as saucers and his nose was as long as a poker.

First the youngest billy-goat crossed the bridge – TRIP TRAP.

'Who's that crossing my bridge?' roared the Troll.

'It's only the smallest billy-goat Gruff. I'm going up the hill to eat grass and grow fat,' said the billy-goat in a tiny voice.

'I shall gobble you up!' roared the Troll.

'Oh, don't do that. My brother is coming along and he's much bigger and fatter than I am.'

'All right, be off,' said the Troll.

Not long after the middle-sized billy-goat came along – TRIP TRAP TRIP.

'Who's that crossing my bridge?' roared the Troll.

'It's only the middle-sized billy-goat Gruff. I'm going up the hill to make myself fat,' said the billy-goat.

'I shall gobble you up,' roared the Troll.

'Oh, don't do that. My brother's coming along and he's much bigger and fatter than I am.'

'All right, be off,' said the Troll.

At last here came the biggest billy-goat – TRIP TRAP TRIP TRAP.

'Who's that crossing my bridge?' roared the Troll.

'BIG BILLY-GOAT GRUFF,' shouted the big billy-goat in a big voice.

'I'm coming to gobble you up,' roared the Troll.

'No, YOU'RE NOT!' shouted the big billy-goat. He ran at the Troll and tossed him in the air and threw him into the river. Then he went up the hill to join his two brothers and they ate and ate until they were as fat as fat. And, as far as I know, they're eating still.

Galldora and the Small Reward

BY MODWENA SEDGWICK

Marybell had a rag doll called Galldora, with shoe-button eyes, a sewn-on mouth, and black wool hair. One day Galldora fell out of the dolls' pram into the river . . . Away and away went the rag doll, with her red dress billowing out like a float about her, and her black wool hair streaming behind. Sometimes her head was under the water, and then she could be friendly with the fishes, and sometimes her head bobbed up over the water, and then she could have polite conversation with the dragonflies and the gnats. I wonder if this will go on for ever and ever? she thought. I really won't mind if it does.

But suddenly she was swilled round in a little eddy of water as it flowed swiftly from under a low iron bridge. The waters whirled her and some floating sticks up against great, smooth stones. To Galldora's surprise, there she stopped. Well, thought Galldora, I suppose I could be in a worse place – and now that I am quite jammed up against these stones, with the sticks all about me, it's not so likely that I will sink.

All that night Galldora stayed there, and she was quite happy, watching the stars and listening to the owls. It's all like a lesson, she told herself, like being educated.

Next day she found she did not lack for company. She was visited by an inquisitive trout who had a nibble at her shoes, and then a toad came and hopped all over her, and decided she made a very nice sun-bathing place. Then a

thrush came and had a tug at her eyes, thinking they were
small snails, and later a cocky little chaffinch came and
asked: 'May I please, rag doll, have a piece of your nice
hair? It will just do for my nest.'

'Certainly,' said Galldora, 'just help yourself.' The chaffinch did. He came back time and time again, and worried
at her hair till she wondered if she would have any hair left.
Thinking of nests, Galldora sighed, just one or two sighs,
in a homesick way. I wonder, she began to think, if I will
ever see all the teddy bears and dolls again, and my own
special window-sill?

When the sun was high in the heavens a fisherman came
walking along the river path, and stopped on the bridge.
He leant there for a moment, gazing down at the cool, clear
waters, and wondering about the fish. As he looked his eye
was caught by a piece of red-coloured cloth, all muddled up
in the pile of driftwood against the big stones and the reeds.
He went over and kicked it, in a wondering sort of way,
with the toes of his boots. The red-coloured rag was, of
course, Galldora, and the kick made her legs and arms leap
about.

'Well, well,' said the fisherman, 'a rag doll.' He bent
down and picked Galldora out of the water and he wrung
her out and he sat her up on an iron spike on the railings of
the bridge. 'I suppose some little girl will be looking for
you,' said the fisherman, and being a kind fisherman he ar-
ranged Galldora very comfortably. He put the spike through
the back of her dress and through the back part of her
woolly hair, so that her face was right up, and she looked
straight out and could watch all that was happening. Then
the fisherman tucked her arms one into the other, so they

didn't dangle down. Galldora thought the fisherman was the kindest person she had ever met. He had certainly taken a lot of trouble over her. She stayed there on the railings in the sun, smiling out on the world as she dried.

It was a lovely, all-alone place where Galldora was, and it was full of overhanging green trees and mossy banks. The primroses shone there like stars, and, of course, it was just the place where birds felt very at home. So at home that they were all crowded up, and the nests were just every-where. One lady robin, who had found all the holes and crevices already full of other birds' nests, came flying over to the bridge, and perched there, looking about for a home. As her bright, beady eyes were flickering this way and that, they met Galldora's bright, shoe-button eyes.

'Oh, dear, you do look worried,' said Galldora.

'Yes, I am,' said the lady robin, 'very worried.'

'What is the matter?' asked Galldora.

'Well, it's this way,' explained the lady robin, 'I can't find anywhere to make my nest. Everywhere is full up this year.'

'Oh, could I – well, if you didn't think I was interfering – make a suggestion?' said Galldora timidly. The lady robin cocked her head on one side to listen. 'You see my arms?' said Galldora. 'They are tucked up, aren't they?'

'Yes,' said the lady robin.

'Well,' said Galldora, still very timidly, 'come and have a closer look.' The lady robin flew over and, perch-ing on Galldora's head, looked at Galldora's tucked-up arms.

'Why!' said the lady robin, 'what a wonderful cosy place to make a nest. It's just what I'm looking for,' and she flew

away and came back a little later with her husband. At once
they started to build a nest in Galldora's arms.

Now, some days later, the fisherman passed Marybell's
house. Outside, on a little tree, he saw a notice hanging by
some string, and the notice said: LOST – A RAG DOLL.
LOST IN RIVER. IF FOUND, SMALL REWARD. He at once
rang the bell and told Marybell's mother all about Galldora.

So, that afternoon, Marybell and her mother went down
to the lonely, greeny part of the river where very few people
went, except fishermen, and there, on the bridge, just as
they had been told, they found Galldora. There too they
found in Galldora's arms a nest with four eggs.

Marybell's mother, who understood all about eggs and
nests, took Marybell a little way away, and they both sat
very silent on the river bank and watched. Quite soon the
lady robin came flying straight to Galldora and sat in the
nest. Marybell was so excited she wanted to jump up and
pick up the eggs, but her mother said:

'No, Marybell, you will upset her, but we'll come every day to see the robin.' So every day Marybell came and looked at Galldora and the robins, from a safe distance, of course, so as not to upset the robins. And every day, when she left, Marybell waved her hand at Galldora. And every day Galldora seemed to wink back.

Marybell was so proud of Galldora she said: 'You know, Mummy, I think Galldora is the cleverest of all my dolls. I think she must have the small reward that the fisherman didn't want.' So Galldora, when the baby robins had grown up and flown away, and she had come home, was given the small reward, which was a diamond star brooch out of a cracker. And Galldora proudly wears it, even to this day.

From *Adventures of Galldora*

Blackie's Birthday

BY DORIS RUST

One day Jane said to her little black dog: 'Blackie, do you know that today is your birthday?'

'Woof!' replied Blackie, 'woof! woof!' and he jumped up and down, wagging not only his tail but almost the whole of his black, furry body.

'You're two years old today,' Jane told him.

'Woof! woof!' said Blackie.

Then he stopped jumping up and down and began to sniff the air. 'Sniff! sniff!' he went, twitching his round black nose, which looked like a little piece of leather. 'Sniff! sniff!'

'He can smell his birthday present, Mummy,' laughed Jane, and she held more tightly a little parcel wrapped in brown paper.

Blackie put his nose on the parcel and then he tried to take it away in his mouth.

'No,' said Jane. 'No, Blackie. You mustn't snatch. Sit down. Sit.'

Blackie sat.

'Stay!'

Blackie stayed quite still. Jane put the parcel on the ground in front of him.

'All right!' she said. 'Open it!'

Blackie pulled the string off with his teeth. Then, making little growling noises, he bit the brown paper away, piece by piece. 'Gr . . . gr . . . gr . . .' he went, until all the paper was torn away. You would never guess what he found inside. It was something that was his favourite thing to eat, something which he only had on his birthday or at Christmas. It was . . . *a cold sausage*!

No sooner had he found it than he gobbled it up just as fast as he could. Jane and her mother picked up the pieces of brown paper and string and threw them in the rubbish box.

'Blackie did enjoy his present,' smiled Mummy. 'As it's his birthday, I think he ought to do what he likes best of all, don't you?'

'And what he likes best of all,' said Jane, 'is going on the common and jumping into the pond.'

'Fetch your lead, Blackie!' said Mummy.

Blackie ran to the door where his lead hung from a hook. He pulled the lead from the hook and brought it to Jane and her mother so that they could fasten it to his collar. Then they all went out of the house and up the road towards the common.

As soon as they were away from all the cars and lorries and bicycles, Jane undid Blackie's lead and let him run. The first thing he did was to race as fast as he could towards the pond. 'Splosh! Splosh!' He was in the water. He swam across to the other side, and then he turned round and swam back again. But this time Jane and her mother had reached the pond and they saw him coming out of the water. He looked very small and thin because his fur was all stuck together. They ran a little way away so that he should not shake all the wetness over *them*!

Blackie shook himself and rolled on the grass to get dry. After they had walked a little farther, Jane said:

'I think Blackie would like to play hide-and-seek.'

'I'm sure he would,' Mummy agreed. 'You go and hide while Blackie and I shut our eyes.'

Mummy sat down beside Blackie and she held her hands over his eyes so that he could not see where Jane was running.

'Cuckoo!' called Jane. 'Cuckoo.'

Mummy took her hands away from Blackie. He looked first this way, then that way.

'Where's Jane?' Mummy asked him. 'Where's Jane?'

Blackie lifted his long ears and put his head on one side. He *loved* playing hide-and-seek.

'Where's Jane?' Mummy asked him.

Off he went, scurrying over the grass, looking first behind one tree, then behind another tree.

'Cuckoo!' called Jane. 'Cuckoo!'

Her voice sounded quite near now. Blackie ran and looked behind a big, green bush and . . . *there* was Jane! He was so pleased to see her that he almost knocked her over.

They played hide-and-seek for a long while. Sometimes Jane hid and sometimes Mummy hid. But Blackie always did the finding. He would not go away and hide by himself because he did not want to leave them.

That evening, after tea, Jane found a piece of blue ribbon which Mummy said she did not want. Jane put it through Blackie's collar and tied it in a bow.

'There!' she said. 'Now you're a birthday dog with a pretty bow.'

But Blackie didn't like the blue bow at all. He waggled his head and he waggled his neck until he could reach the bow with his mouth. Then he pulled it undone. Every time Jane made a nice new bow, Blackie untied it with his teeth. And then, at last, when Jane wasn't looking, he pulled it right off and chewed it into little pieces.

'Oh! Blackie!' said Jane.

'Never mind!' Mummy said, 'Blackie just doesn't feel comfortable in a bow. And I really think he's getting rather tired. Let's say good night to him before we turn on your bath water.'

Blackie was already creeping into his basket and curling himself into a ball. Jane patted his furry head. 'Good night, Blackie-dog,' she said, softly.

Blackie opened one eye and gave a long, happy sigh. Ah – a – a – ah! What a day! He had had a cold sausage as well as his ordinary dinner. He had jumped into the pond. He had played hide-and-seek on the common. And he had torn a silly blue bow into little pieces. He had had a *lovely* birthday.

From *A Story a Day*

Clocks and Watches

Our great
Steeple clock
Goes TICK-TOCK,
TICK-TOCK;

Our small
Mantel clock
Goes TICK-TACK, TICK-TACK,
TICK-TACK, TICK-TACK;

Our little
Pocket-watch
Goes Tick-a-tacker, tick-a-tacker,
Tick-a-tacker, tick.

ANONYMOUS

Christmas

BY VERA M. COLWELL

It was Christmas Eve, and David and Cynthia were busy wrapping presents. There was a piece of pink scented soap and a kettle holder that Cynthia had knitted for Mummy, and a note-book and a handkerchief for Daddy.

'Don't look, David,' said Cynthia, trying to wrap up the signal she had bought for his train set. It was so nobbly and the sharp edges would keep poking through the paper. She was afraid David would guess what it was before Christmas Day.

David was only four so he had to ask Mummy to help him to wrap up Cynthia's present, a book he and Mummy had chosen for her.

'There!' said Cynthia at last. 'The presents are all ready for the Christmas tree.'

'Come on,' said David impatiently. 'Let's see if Daddy has finished the fairy lights on the tree.'

They picked up their parcels and ran into the next room. It was all in darkness, but suddenly as they stood at the door, the lights came on all over the tree, red, yellow, orange, and blue. The strings of silver tinsel glittered, the icicles sparkled and, right on the top of the tree, a light shone on a doll-angel with its wings outspread.

'How lovely!' exclaimed Cynthia. 'It's so bright and sparkly.'

'Can I switch the lights off and on, Daddy?' asked David. He loved to do this now that he could reach the switches.

'Just once,' said Daddy, 'and then off you go to bed.'

'David! Cynthia!' called Mummy. 'Time for bed.'

'Oh, Mummy! Can we just tie our presents on the tree, please?

'Of course,' said Mummy, 'but don't be long. You mustn't be late to bed tonight because it is Christmas to-morrow.'

Daddy helped the two children to tie their parcels on the prickly branches of the tree and then they ran off upstairs.

Washed and in their pyjamas, David and Cynthia sat up in bed. Mummy had brought their supper up to them for a treat.

'Listen quietly,' began Mummy, 'and I'll tell you the Christmas story.'

While they sat quietly, she told them about the shepherds in the fields with their sheep, and the Angels singing, and how the Baby Jesus was born in the stable at Bethlehem, and how the Star led the Wise Men to worship Him and bring Him presents.

'Is the Star in the sky tonight?' asked Cynthia.

'Perhaps, but you must cuddle down now and go to sleep. Remember that Father Christmas likes to find children asleep when he comes with their presents.'

'I don't think my stocking is going to be big enough,' said David anxiously. 'I've asked Father Christmas for a tricycle and it won't go in a stocking.'

'I asked for a doll's pram,' said Cynthia. 'What will Father Christmas do about big things like that?'

'Don't worry,' said Mummy smiling. 'Wait and see.' She switched off the light and went downstairs.

'Let's watch for Father Christmas coming,' whispered David.

'My friend Pauline says she has never seen him,' said Cynthia, 'and she's quite old, nearly ten.'

They crept out of bed and peeped round the edge of the curtains. The stars were shining and the frost on the ground sparkled like the tinsel on the Christmas tree. But nothing moved in the night sky.

'Can you see him?' asked David.

There was a sudden bump and clatter in the next room. 'Is that him?' exclaimed Cynthia. 'Perhaps he's come down the wrong chimney!'

They ran across the landing and peeped into their parents' room. Suddenly something soft rubbed against their legs.

'Ph, puss, you naughty cat!' said Cynthia. 'You've been on Mummy's dressing table again and knocked off her hair-brush.'

'Children, where are you?' called Mummy. 'What's that noise?'

'It's just Pussy. We thought we heard Father Christmas in the chimney, Mummy.'

'Into bed this minute,' said their mother and tucked them up again. Soon their cold feet were warm and the two children fell fast asleep.

The stars were still shining and the night was very quiet when the children were wakened by the sound of singing outside their window. It was the carol singers:

'Away in a manger, no crib for a bed,
 The little Lord Jesus laid down His sweet head,'

Only half awake, they turned over:

'The stars in the bright sky looked down where He lay,
 The little Lord Jesus asleep on the hay.'

Then they were asleep once more and dreaming of the Baby, stars, shining Christmas trees, angels, and presents.

When they awoke again it was early morning. 'Is it time to get up?' asked David sleepily.

'Wake up, David, it's Christmas Day!' said Cynthia. She switched on the light and looked at the foot of the bed. Yes, Father Christmas had been. Their stockings were so fat that they were nearly falling off the bed.

They began to explore their stockings – an apple, an orange, sweets, a bar of chocolate, and some small exciting parcels.

'I'm going to show Mummy,' David got out of his bed.

'It's only half past six,' said Cynthia importantly. She could tell the time now and she wasn't sure that Daddy and Mummy would want to be wakened up yet.

But David was halfway across the landing already, so Cynthia ran after him and they both called 'Merry Christmas! Father Christmas has been!'

They climbed up on to their parents' bed and began to chatter.

'Shall I tell you what I've got for you, Daddy?' whispered David.

'You mustn't tell, David! It's a surprise. Mummy, you'll never guess what I've made for you!'

'How exciting, darlings!' said Mummy. 'When can we see our presents?'

'I'll fetch them now,' said Cynthia kindly. 'Come on, David.'

David slid down from the bed and then hesitated. 'Daddy,' he said slowly, 'I asked Father Christmas for a tricycle. It's not here . . .'

'And my doll's pram,' said Cynthia remembering.

'Maybe he couldn't carry them upstairs?' suggested Daddy. 'Quick, put on your dressing-gowns and slippers and have a look downstairs.'

The children dashed across to their bedroom, pulled on their dressing-gowns and slippers, and hurried down the stairs, nearly falling over Pussy who was coming up to see what all the excitement was about.

There in the hall stood a tricycle painted red and blue and a green doll's pram with a white hood.

'Oh!' cried the children, almost speechless with wonder.

'My tricycle's got a bell!' said David, ringing it loudly. 'Oh, lucky me!'

'Look at this furry little pram-rug!' said Cynthia, stroking it lovingly. 'Mummy! Daddy! Come and see what Father Christmas has brought us.'

'Hurrah! for Christmas Day in the morning,' shouted the children as their parents came down the stairs.

'And lots more fun to come!' said Mummy, for this was only the beginning of David and Cynthia's happy Christmas. There was still all kinds of excitement to look forward to – the Christmas tree, Christmas dinner, Christmas cake, games, and fun. But that is another story.

The Tale of a Turnip

BY ELIZABETH CLARK

Once upon a time there was a little old Man, and a little old Woman his wife, and a little Girl their grandchild, and a little black-and-white Cat, and a little Mouse (that lived where nobody knew but only the little black-and-white Cat): and they all lived together in a little house.

One day the little old Man said to the little old Woman his wife, 'I'm going out to the field to plant a seed,' and she said, 'What kind of a seed?' and he said, 'A turnip seed.' So the little old Man went out to the field, and he dug a little hole, and he put in a seed (and it *was* a turnip seed), and he went back to the house and said to the little old Woman, 'I've planted it!' And they both said, 'We hope it will grow.'

And it did grow. The sun shone and the wind blew and the rain rained, and a little green shoot came out of the ground, and it grew, and it grew, and it grew, and it *grew* till it grew to a very big turnip (as big as this!). So one day when it was grown (as big as this) the little old Man said to the little old Woman his wife, 'Put the pot on the fire and boil some water, and mind it's a big pot, for I'm going to pull up the turnip and we'll all have turnip soup.'

So the little old Woman made up the fire and took the biggest pot she had and filled it with water, and put it on the fire to boil the water to make the turnip soup. And the little old Man went out to the field and he caught hold of the turnip, and he pulled, and he pulled, and he pulled, and he *pulled*, but he couldn't pull up the turnip.

So the little old Man called to the little old Woman his wife, 'Come and take hold of me, that we may pull up the turnip.'

So the little old Woman his wife left the pot boiling on the fire, and she came running out of the house; and the little old Woman his wife had hold of the little old Man her husband, and the little old Man her husband had hold of the turnip; and they pulled, and they pulled, and they pulled, and they *pulled*, but they couldn't pull up the turnip.

So the little old Woman his wife called to the little Girl their grandchild and said, 'Come and take hold of me, that we may pull up the turnip.'

So the little Girl their grandchild came running out of the house; and the little Girl the grandchild had hold of the little old Woman the grandmother, and the little old Woman the grandmother had hold of the little old Man her husband, and the little old Man her husband had hold of the turnip; and they pulled, and they pulled, and they pulled, and they *pulled*, but they couldn't pull up the turnip.

So the little Girl the grandchild called to the little black-and-white Cat, and said, 'Come and take hold of me, that we may pull up the turnip.'

So the little black-and-white Cat came running out of the house (with its tail in the air, as little cats do when they're pleased); and the little black-and-white Cat had hold of the little Girl the grandchild, and the little Girl the grandchild had hold of the little old Woman the grandmother, and the little old Woman the grandmother had hold of the little old Man her husband, and the little old Man her husband had hold of the turnip; and they pulled, and they pulled, and they pulled, and they *pulled*, but they couldn't pull up the turnip.

So the little black-and-white Cat called to the little Mouse (that lived where nobody knew but only the little black-and-white Cat) and said, 'Come and take hold of me, that we may pull up the turnip.'

So the little Mouse *popped* out of its hole (that nobody knew but only the little black-and-white Cat); and the little Mouse had hold of the little black-and-white Cat, the little black-and-white Cat had hold of the little Girl the grandchild, the little Girl the grandchild had hold of the little old Woman the grandmother, and the little old Woman the grandmother

had hold of the little old Man her husband, and the little old Man her husband had hold of the turnip; and they pulled, and they pulled, and they pulled, and they pulled, and *up* came the turnip! But the little old Man fell over on top of the little old Woman his wife, and the little old Woman his wife fell over on top of the little Girl the grandchild, and the little Girl the grandchild fell over on top of the little black-and-white Cat, and the little black-and-white Cat fell over on top of the little Mouse (that lived where nobody knew but only the little black-and-white Cat), and on top of them all was the turnip!

But nobody was hurt, and it was a very good turnip, and it made very good turnip soup. There was enough for the little old Man, and the little old Woman his wife, and the little Girl the grandchild, and the little black-and-white Cat, *and* the little Mouse (that lived where nobody knew but only the little black-and-white Cat) – and there was enough left over for the person who told the story!

From *Stories to Tell and How to Tell Them*

Marmaduke is Frozen

BY ELIZABETH CHAPMAN

It was a bitterly cold day. As Marmaduke the lorry and Joe
rode over the hills from Manchester on their way home, Joe
had to keep stopping to take off his gloves, so that he could
blow on his hands to keep them warm. His gloves were very
thick and lined with fleecy wool, but they weren't warm
enough to keep out the biting frost.

'My word, Marmaduke,' he said, 'I've never known it as
cold as this. Look at those icicles on that waterfall. I *shall* be
glad when we're home tonight.'

'Yes, I'm cold too,' said Marmaduke. 'Let's have a song, Joe. That may make us warmer.'

So Joe sang:

> 'Merrily we go,
> Marmaduke and Joe,
> Singing high and low,
> Merrily we go.'

And Marmaduke said 'Toot-toot' on his horn as loudly as he could.

On they rode and on they sang, and colder and colder it grew. Then suddenly: 'Oh dear!' Marmaduke said, 'Oh dear me! Oh, Joe, my back tyre! Oh, I shall have to stop!'

Joe pulled up quickly.

'Why, what is it, Marmaduke?'

'Oh, Joe!' he gasped. 'I think my tyre's punctured.'

'Let's have a look,' said Joe, and out he got and walked round to the back of the lorry to have a look.

In a few seconds he was back.

'I'm afraid you're right,' he said. 'And on such a cold night, too. Never mind,' he added kindly, as he saw how miserable the lorry was looking. 'I'll change the wheel for you, and then we'll be on our way again. I'll be as quick as I can.'

So Joe got out his tools, and soon had the spare wheel off the back. Then he took out the jack, and started to lift up the back of the lorry so that he could take off the wheel with the punctured tyre. By this time his hands were so cold that he could hardly move them. He had to keep stopping and smacking them together to try to bring some life into them.

'I d-don't want to sound imp-p-patient,' said Marmaduke.

He was shivering so much that he could scarcely speak. 'But I'm getting c-colder and c-colder, Joe.'

'I'm working as fast as I can, old chap,' said Joe. 'But my hands keep going numb ... Oh dear, this *would* have to happen.'

'Hello, is anything wrong?'

Joe jumped at the sound of another voice. He hadn't heard the man ride up on his bicycle. He explained what had happened, and was so pleased when the man offered to help. They took it in turns to unscrew the bolts, and take off the wheel. While one was working, the other would stamp about and fling his arms round his body to keep himself warm. Then they would change places, and after some time the spare wheel was safely in place.

'Thank you very much for your help,' said Joe to the man. 'Perhaps we can give you a lift home.'

'That's very kind of you,' replied the man. 'I've rather a long way to go yet and I believe you go right past my house, so I should be so grateful if you could take me along with you. It's very cold riding a bicycle in this weather.'

So he lifted his bicycle into the back of the lorry, and then climbed in beside Joe.

'There,' said Marmaduke's master. 'Now, then, off we go, Marmaduke. Soon be home now,' and he pressed the self-starter.

Nothing happened. Joe pressed it again. Still nothing happened.

'I expect it's with him being so cold,' Joe explained to the man. 'We'll try the starting-handle.'

So Joe got out of the lorry, and went to the front to start the engine that way.

'Drer-rer-rer,' went the handle. And then silence. 'Drer-rer-rer.' Still silence. 'Drer-rer-rer.' Silence again.

'Here, let me have a try,' said the man. 'You're probably tired.'

'Drer-rer-rer. Drer-rer-rer. Drer-rer-rer.'

'Oh dear!' sighed Marmaduke. 'What is wrong with me? Oh, I'm so cold. I feel like the blocks of ice the fishmonger has on his slab.'

'Now don't worry,' said Joe. 'I think I know what's happened. This may shock you a little, but I think the water in your radiator has frozen solid. And it's all my fault,' he added sadly. 'I've been meaning to put in some special mixture to stop you freezing up, but somehow I've never had time. Oh, I *do* wish I had. This would never have happened then. Oh well, we shall just have to thaw out.'

But Joe and the man looked sadly at each other. How were they going to thaw him out on such a night?

'I've never known that happen to a lorry or a car in such a short time,' said Joe. 'We couldn't have been more than half an hour changing that wheel.'

'And I've never known such icy weather,' said the man. 'It's like the North Pole here tonight.'

'Oh well, perhaps a polar bear will come and sit on me and thaw me out,' said Marmaduke. He felt he had to say something funny because Joe looked so worried and unhappy.

'That's an idea!' said Joe. 'We'll sit on his radiator, and see if the warmth of our bodies will melt the ice.'

So Joe sat on top of the bonnet, and the man – he said his name was Mike – pressed himself up against the radiator front as tightly as he could.

They stayed there for fully ten minutes, but by that time they were both so cold Marmaduke could feel them shaking.

'I'm n-not f-feeling any warmer,' said Marmaduke. 'But do t-try again.'

So Joe got the starting-handle again.

'Drer-rer-rer, drer-rer-rer, drer-rer-rer,' but nothing happened.

'It's no good,' said Marmaduke. 'You'll just have to let this gentleman go home, Joe, and we'll have to stay here all night. Perhaps the sun will shine in the morning and melt the ice.'

'We can't do that,' said Joe. 'But what are we going to do?'

'I've got a shed at my house,' said Mike. 'If we could get him there, you could stay with me tonight. At least, we'd be out of this icy wind, and we could probably thaw him out with some hot water.'

'Yes, but how can we get him there?' sighed Joe. 'Oh well, let's sit inside the cab where it's a little warmer, and try to think of a way.'

They sat and thought and thought for some time, and then suddenly: 'Look!' shouted Joe. 'Here's something coming.'

Sure enough, two small lights were coming along the road from behind them. The lights got larger and larger, and then a big car drew up beside them.

'What's wrong?' asked the man who was driving. 'Can I help?'

'My lorry's frozen up,' explained Joe. 'We're trying to think of a way to get him to this gentleman's house, but it's several miles away, and we can't think how we can do it.'

'Oh, we'll soon fix that,' said the man. 'I've got a rope in the back. Always carry one with me. Never know what's going to happen. I'll give you a tow. Come on, give me a hand. Mustn't stop long or *I* shall be frozen up.'

Very soon Marmaduke was tied to the back of the car, and away they went along the road.

Slowly they drove along, and by and by they arrived at Mike's house, and soon Marmaduke was in the dry shed away from the biting wind, and Joe and Mike were thanking the driver of the car and waving good-bye as he went on his way home.

After Marmaduke had had some hot water poured into his radiator, and rugs wrapped round him, he stopped shaking, and a warm glow began to creep over him.

'Now, then,' said Joe briskly. 'I'll just pour another jugful of water into you, and then I'll try and start your engine.'

So Joe poured in the water, and after waiting a little while for it to melt the ice he climbed into the driving seat and pressed the self-starter.

Marmaduke's engine purred like a contented cat.

'That's done the trick,' said Joe. 'You're not a block of ice on a fishmonger's slab any longer, Marmaduke.'

Marmaduke was glad to hear this. How warm he was now. It made him feel warm, too, to know that there were such kind people in the world as Mike and the man with the car.

'Good night, Joe,' he said, and fell fast asleep.

Next morning he and Joe were able to continue on their way home, none the worse for their adventure.

From *Merry Marmaduke*

Motor-car Game

My motor is humming,
I'm coming, I'm coming,
Make room, make room, make room!
Not a minute to wait,
I'm late, I'm late,
Make room, make room, make room!

MONA SWANN

Teddy Bear Coalman

BY PHOEBE AND SELBY WORTHINGTON

Once upon a time there was a Teddy Bear Coalman who lived all by himself. He had a horse, a cart, and some little bags of coal.

He had a little alarm clock which woke him early every morning, except on Sundays and holidays.

After breakfast, the Teddy Bear Coalman said to his horse, 'Gee-up, Horse!' and the horse went down the road, clippety-CLOP, clippety-CLOP, until they came to a house.

The Teddy Bear Coalman knocked at the door and the lady who answered it said, 'Three bags, please.' So he went to his cart and got a bag of coal on his back.

He threw it into the lady's coal shed. BANG! it went. And another bag. BANG! And yet another bag. BANG! The lady gave him three pennies, which he put in his pocket – one, two, three.

Then he got on his cart again and said to his horse. 'Gee-up, Horse!' and the horse went down the road again, clippety-CLOP, clippety-CLOP, until they came to another house.

This time the lady said, 'Two bags, please,' so the Teddy Bear Coalman put two bags of coal in her shed – BANG!! BANG!!

Then he said to the lady, 'Two pennies, please,' and the lady gave him two pennies, which he put in his pocket – one, two. Then he got on his cart again and the horse went to more houses down the road, clippety-CLOP, clippety-CLOP, until all the coal had gone.

146

Then he said to his horse, 'Home, Horse!' and the horse
turned round and went along the road as fast as he could
clippety-clop, clippety-clop, clippety-clop, clippety-clop.

When they got home, the horse had his tea, and the Teddy
Bear Coalman had his tea. He sat in front of the fire, looking
at pictures in a book.

Then he yawned and went upstairs, undressed all by himself, got into his little cot and soon he was fast asleep.

And that is the story of Teddy Bear Coalman.

From *Teddy Bear Coalman*

Finger Play

Two little dicky birds sat upon a wall,
   (*Show first fingers*)
One named Peter, one named Paul,
Fly away Peter, fly away Paul,
   (*Put one finger, then the other behind your back*)
Come back Peter, come back Paul.
   (*Let them return one at a time*)

TRADITIONAL

A Fit of the Sulks

BY MARGARET LAW

Wendy was in the sulks. She was very cross because Daddy had taken Tommy out without her.

'I'm sorry, Wendy,' Daddy said, 'but little girls with sniffles like yours are better indoors on a cold day like this. Be good and take your cough-mixture, and perhaps you'll be well enough to come out with us tomorrow.'

But Wendy would not take her cough-mixture. When Mother came to give it to her, she shut her lips tightly, put her hands behind her back, and shook her head firmly.

'Come now, Wendy,' said Mother. 'It doesn't taste as bad as all that. Be a brave girl. Open your mouth wide, and it will be over before you can wink.'

But Wendy would not do it.

Puss came into the room – pat-a-pat pat on her soft little paws. She sat down and washed her whiskers.

'Look at Puss,' said Mother. 'She takes her medicine without any fuss. She had a big spoonful of olive oil this morning to make her coat shine. Surely you won't let Puss beat you.'

But Wendy would not open her mouth.

Floppy the spaniel came into the room – flip, flap, flippetty-flap on his feathery feet.

'Look at Floppy,' said Mother. 'He takes his medicine without any fuss. He had a powder in a butter ball this morning to make his coat shine. Surely you won't let a little dog beat you.'

But Wendy would not open her mouth.

Just then Joey the budgerigar began to sing – 'Trill, trill, trill. Trill, trill, trill.'

'Look at Joey,' said Mother. 'He takes his medicine without any fuss. He had some in his water this morning, and drank up every drop of it. Surely you won't let a little bird beat you.'

But Wendy would not open her mouth.

'Tommy hasn't got to take medicine,' she said, 'so why should I do it?'

'Tommy hasn't got a cold,' said Mother, 'and you have. When Tommy had toothache the dentist didn't pull out your tooth as well as Tommy's one. That's a very silly way to talk.'

Now Wendy knew that that was true, but she hadn't quite got over her sulks, so she said, 'I haven't got a cold. At least, it's better now.'

Would you believe it? – the words were hardly out of her mouth when she gave a great big sneeze! She was so astonished that her mouth fell open, and before she could shut it again Mother had popped the spoon inside it. Down Wendy's throat went the cough-mixture before she could do a thing to stop it.

'There now,' said Mother. 'Fancy making a fuss about that,' and off she went to wash the spoon.

Puss and Floppy sat up and looked at Wendy as if they were thinking, 'At last you're being sensible.'

Puss rubbed against her legs, and Floppy jumped up and put his paws on her dress.

'You're a good girl now,' they seemed to be saying, and inside herself Wendy felt very much better.

From *Stories to Tell to the Nursery*

Sarah the Lamb

BY VERA M. COLWELL

Sarah was a little white woolly lamb who lived in a field with her mother and her two sisters. There were other lambs, too, some black, some with white head or feet, and some white all over like Sarah. Her mother was kind and gentle and loved her lambs.

One day Sarah decided to go round the field on her own. She had walked a little way with her mother several times, but not very far. So, when her mother was busy eating grass, she slipped away.

She was only two weeks old and her legs were rather long and thin, but she trotted off feeling very brave.

Sarah made her way along by the hedge as quickly as she could so that her sister lambs would not see and follow her. Through a gap in the hedge she could see into the next field where some creatures, much larger than herself, were busy feeding. Sarah didn't know what they were, but she stayed on her side of the hedge to be safe.

She had only just started off again when something sprang in front of her out of a hole in the bank. Sarah jumped in the air with fright, landing on her four little feet in time to hear a voice say, 'Hello, little lamb. What are you doing all alone?'

'Oh,' said Sarah, 'I'm going round the field all by myself. I'm not really so little, you know.'

'Aren't you?' said the rabbit. 'Well, take care, that's all I say, for some queer creatures come this way sometimes.'

The rabbit ran away like the wind. 'I wonder who that was?' thought Sarah.

She went on a little more slowly and carefully until she came to a gate. She tried to push her head through the bars but they were covered with wire. She poked her black nose through and smelt the air. There was no field out there, only a hard white road. Suddenly she heard a whirring noise and then – swish – something large and dark shot past her, nearly touching her nose.

She ran away from the gate in fear. When she stopped again and looked back timidly towards the road, the car had gone. 'I wonder what that was?' thought Sarah.

She was beginning to think it would be better to go back to her mother, but the pale March sunshine made her feel happy again. 'Perhaps I'll just go across the field and see what I meet there,' she said to herself.

Several lambs were running over the field and forming into a line. 'Are you going to have a race?' she called. 'Can I join in?' They looked round at her. 'Hurry up!' they answered. 'We're off!' Sarah had just time to join the lambs when off they went, racing and skipping over the grass.

Up a hillock and down the other side they ran, then all of a sudden they stopped, turned round, and started back again. Sarah was soon left behind for her little legs were tired. All the lambs scampered back to their mothers.

But where was Sarah's mother? 'What are you doing by yourself?' asked a little black lamb. 'You are too young to be away from your mother.'

'Oh, I'm not so very young really,' said Sarah.

'Well, be careful,' said the black lamb. 'My mother says a fox comes this way sometimes.'

Sarah suddenly felt very much alone. The pale March sun had gone in and the rain began to fall. The other lambs sheltered by their mothers, but when Sarah ran up to a mother sheep, she was pushed away.

'Ma-aa,' said Sarah in a sad little voice, and then she said 'Ma-aa' again, this time a little louder. But there was no answer. Where could mother be?

'I wish I had stayed at home,' said Sarah. The wind blew harder so that she could hardly stand up. She ran about trying to find somewhere to shelter but the field was big and empty.

Then she heard a soft, far-away 'Baa-aa.' It was her mother's voice. 'Ma-aa,' she cried as loudly as she could.

'Ba-aa,' came the voice again. With a leap and a bound Sarah ran forward and there was her mother. How glad she was to see her once more.

Sarah crept under her mother crying softly 'Ma-aa. I am glad you found me. I won't run away again!' Her mother pushed her farther under her strong woolly self. 'Baa-aa,' she said in a comforting tone. 'Silly little lamb, you are safe now.'

Thomas the Kitten Goes to the Country

BY URSULA HOURIHANE

Thomas the Kitten lived in a big, noisy, dirty town. Thomas didn't know it was big and noisy and dirty. He had never lived anywhere else, and he was so used to hearing buses hooting and cars honking and people shouting that he never thought about it. And then one day Thomas was prowling about in the street outside his house when a large van pulled by a big brown horse stopped just beside him. On the side of the van was a beautiful picture of the country-side. There were green fields, tall trees, a sparkling little stream, a dear little white cottage with flowers in the garden, and all sorts of other nice things in the picture. Thomas looked and looked.

'That must be a funny place,' he said to himself. 'There aren't any buses or cars or people anywhere. Wherever can it be? I think it looks a nice place. I wish I knew how I could get there.'

He looked again at the picture and he saw the sky was bright blue – not all grey and tired-looking like the sky above his town. And he saw there were birds flying up in the air and perched on the branches of the trees – not just hopping about in the dust of the street as they did in his town. And then he looked closer still and he saw – sitting on the step of the little white cottage, between the rows of pretty flowers and right in the middle of a patch of warm sunshine – a small tabby kitten, just like himself! Thomas the Kitten was surprised!

'Well,' he said, 'that kitten is lucky. He's living in such a dear little white house and he has plenty of space to play in and the sun is shining in such a blue sky. I do wish I knew where it was. I wonder if the horse could tell me how to get there.'

He skipped round to the front of the van and looked up at the big brown horse. 'Please,' he said, as loudly as he could with all the noise of the buses and cars and people all around. 'Please, Horse, could you tell me how to get to that lovely place in the picture on your van?'

The big brown horse looked down in surprise. 'Whatever do you want to go there for?' he said. 'That's the country. It's very quiet. The town's much more interesting, little kitten.'

'I think it looks a lovely place,' said Thomas the Kitten. 'And I want to go and see for myself.'

'Oh well, if you really insist,' said the big brown horse, 'I can give you a lift part of the way. Jump up and hide among the parcels in my van. I'll take you as far as I can.'

'Thank you,' said Thomas the Kitten gladly. And he jumped up into the van and snuggled down among the parcels, making himself as small as he could.

Presently the driver of the van came back, climbed into his seat again, called 'Gee up, there!' to the big brown horse, and away they went—clippety-clop, clippety-clop, rumble, rumble.

It was dark and stuffy inside the van and Thomas the Kitten began to feel sleepy. He yawned and stretched. Then he curled himself into a little ball and went fast asleep. The van and the big brown horse went on and on – clippety-clop, clippety-clop, rumble, rumble.

At last nearly all the parcels had been delivered. The driver got down with a big box and went off to a house. The big brown horse called out, 'Hey there, little kitten! You'd better get down now or the driver will find you. There are hardly any parcels left and we're nearly in the country. Wake up. Wake up.'

Thomas the Kitten blinked his eyes. Then he yawned and stretched. Then suddenly he felt wide awake again. He remembered where he was and how he was going to see the lovely place in the picture. He skipped out of the stuffy van and jumped lightly to the ground.

'Thank you so much, Horse,' he said politely. 'That was a lovely drive. Is this the country place you said?'

'Not quite, little kitten,' said the horse. 'But I'm sure you can find someone here who will tell you how to get there. Ask that horse in the baker's van. He looks sensible and kind. He's sure to know.'

Thomas the Kitten thanked the big brown horse again and went to see the baker's horse. He looked to the right and to the left, but there wasn't anything coming along the road anywhere. Thomas was surprised. He had never seen such an empty road in his big, noisy, dirty town. He ran across and looked up at the baker's horse.

'Please, Baker's Horse,' he said as loud as he could, because he forgot there were no buses or cars or people here to make a noise, 'Please, Baker's Horse, could you tell me how I can get to the country?'

The baker's horse looked very surprised. 'Don't shout so,' he said. 'I'm not deaf, you know, little kitten. I'm going down to a village in the country now. If you like to hop in the back I'll give you a lift.'

'Thank you,' said Thomas the Kitten in a nice gentle little voice. And he jumped up into the baker's cart and snuggled down in a dark corner. Presently the baker came back, climbed into his seat again, called 'Gee up there!' to his horse, and away they went, clippety-clop, clippety-clop, rumble, rumble. Sometimes the baker stopped the cart and got down to take some bread and cakes and buns to the cottages on the way. Then Thomas the Kitten used to peep out to see where they were. It all looked lovely, he thought, but the baker's horse said, 'Wait a little longer. We're not quite there yet.'

At last when the baker had jumped down and taken his basket of good things through a small white gate, the horse called out, 'Hi! little kitten, you'd better get down now before he comes back. We're nearly in the village and there will be more people about, and perhaps dogs.' Thomas the Kitten skipped out of his dark corner and jumped lightly to the ground.

'Thank you so much, Baker's Horse,' he said politely. 'That was a lovely ride.' Then he skipped quickly behind a big tree at the edge of the road because he heard the baker coming back and he didn't want to be seen. Off went the baker's horse and cart – clippety-clop, clippety-clop, rumble, rumble.

Thomas the Kitten crept out from behind the tree and peered through the white gate. Then he said, 'OOH!' Inside the white gate there was a path leading to the door of a little white cottage. And on the door-step of the little white cottage sat – can you guess what? Yes, a small tabby kitten – just like Thomas and just like the kitten in the picture. Thomas could hardly believe his eyes. He squeezed gently under the white gate and walked slowly down the path.

'Mew? Mew?' said Thomas the Kitten as he came up to the other little tabby kitten on the door-step.

'Miaou, miaou!' said the other little tabby kitten when she saw Thomas coming.

'Mew! Miaou! Mew! Miaou!' they both said together, and soon they were just like two old friends. Thomas told Tibby, the other kitten, where he came from, and Tibby told Thomas how she lived at the little white cottage with Miss Sarah who loved cats and kittens and would want Thomas to stay, too. And presently, out came Miss Sarah, and when she saw the two kittens having such fun together she begged Thomas to stay and live with them. And, as far as I know, that's where Thomas the Kitten is to this day – playing with Tibby and sniffing the sweet flowers in Miss Sarah's garden, and so happy that he never wants to go back to his big, noisy, dirty town again.

From *Highways and Holidays*

The Pot and the Kettle

'Bubble,' says the Kettle,
'Bubble,' says the Pot.
'Bubble, bubble, bubble!
We are very, very hot.'
'Shall I lift you off the fire?'
'No, you needn't trouble.
That is just the way we talk:
Bubble, bubble, bubble!'

RODNEY BENNETT

All Change!

BY URSULA HOURIHANE

There were once four friends. They were a small ginger kitten, a small white puppy, a little brown rabbit, and a baby rook. They lived in the country and they had all sorts of fun together. Sometimes Baby Rook used to pick off tiny twigs and fir cones and drop them down from his home high up in the trees for Kitten to play with. Sometimes Puppy would roll his little rubber ball right down Rabbit's hole to play with. Sometimes Rabbit would pick a dandelion-clock from the meadow and send the little white fluffets puffing up and up for Baby Rook to catch. Sometimes Kitten would hold her old cotton reel on a string in her sharp white teeth and let Puppy chase it round the garden. They were always thinking of new tricks to play and new things to do. And then, one day, when they had played their old games a hundred times and were sitting around thinking of something quite new to do, Kitten had a great idea.

'I know,' she cried. 'Let's all change houses for one night!'

'Change houses?' squawked Baby Rook.

'Change houses? snuffled Rabbit.

'Change houses?' woofed Puppy.

They all cried together, 'What *do* you mean, Kitten?'

The small ginger kitten looked at them and she said, 'I mean, why shouldn't we all try living in one another's houses? Just for a change, of course, not for ever. I'm a good climber so I'd better go up in Rook's tree.'

'And I'm a good burrower,' said Puppy, 'so I could have a turn in Rabbit's home.'

'I couldn't bear to be shut up indoors,' said Baby Rook, 'so I'd better go in Puppy's box in the stable.'

'And that means I can sleep in Kitten's cosy basket by the fire,' said the little brown rabbit. 'What fun!'

As soon as they saw the sun was setting ready for bed the four little friends all thought they had better begin to settle into their new homes for the night.

Kitten looked up and down the high tree where Baby Rook's nest was tucked in between some twigs, and she wasn't so sure she wanted to sleep there after all. But she didn't like to say so because the others might think she was a cowardly cat. So she called 'Good night!' dug her sharp little claws into the rough bark of the tree, and began to climb.

Puppy looked down Rabbit's dark hole and he wasn't so sure he wanted to sleep there after all. But he didn't want the others to think he was afraid, so he called 'Good night!' and crept into the dark passage that went on and on and out of sight.

Baby Rook fluttered along to the stable where Puppy slept in a box full of straw on the ground. It looked very low down and she thought it might be very dangerous if people should want to tread there. She wasn't so sure she wanted to sleep there after all. But all the others were going to their new homes and she wasn't going to be the only one left out, so she cawed 'Good night!' and hopped into the stable.

The little brown rabbit was left alone. He scuttled over to the back door and poked his head round. There inside, by the fire, was Kitten's basket with a soft cushion in it and a saucer of milk nearby. He didn't much like the idea of having no nice dark corner to huddle in, but he had nowhere else to sleep now, so in he went, plip-plop, plip-plop!

By the time Kitten had scrambled and clawed her way right up to Baby Rook's home, she was quite worn out. It felt very wobbledy and chilly high up there in the tree, but she was too tired to care any more and she curled round and tried to go to sleep.

By the time Puppy had scrambled and bumped his way along the dark stuffy passages to Rabbit's home, he was quite worn out. It felt damp and chilly under the ground, but he was too tired to care any more and he flopped down and tried to go to sleep.

By the time Baby Rook had poked and twisted the straw in Puppy's box into some sort of hollow to snuggle into, she was quite worn out. It felt dusty and hard in the box but she was too tired to care any more. She tucked her head down and tried to go to sleep.

By the time Rabbit had turned the cushion in Kitten's basket this way and that and poked his head underneath to shut out the light from the fire, he was quite worn out. It felt hot and stuffy in the kitchen and he kept hearing strange noises that upset him, but he was really too tired to care any more and he burrowed in as best he could and tried to go to sleep.

Presently the wind rose and the rain began to fall.

Baby Rook's nest swayed to and fro, high up in the tree, Kitten was very frightened. 'MIAOUGH! I'm not staying up here,' she said to herself and she began to hurry down to the ground again.

The rain grew heavier and heavier. Little cold streams of water trickled down Rabbit's passage and made puddles on the earth floor. Puppy was shivering and miserable. 'OO-OW!' he howled sadly. 'I'm not staying here any more.' And he hurried off down the passage to get above ground again.

The wind grew stronger and louder. The stable door creaked and squeaked and began to bang to and fro. Baby Rook was frightened.

'CAA-CAA!' she squawked. 'I'm not staying here. I might get shut in for ever.' And she flew out as fast as she could.

Inside by the fire it was warm enough and Rabbit didn't even know there was a storm blowing. But the fire crackled and spat and a cinder fell out near his fluffy coat. Rabbit was frightened, 'POOFF!' I'm not staying here,' he said to himself. 'I might catch fire!' And he scuttled off as fast as he could go.

In a few minutes the storm was over and a big golden moon came shining out of the clouds. It shone down on the garden and the fields and what did it see? – One small ginger kitten, one small white puppy, one little brown rabbit, and one baby rook! all looking very lost and scared and all surprised to see each other. And it wasn't long, I can tell you, before Kitten was curled up cosily in her basket; Puppy was snuggled down in his box of straw; little brown Rabbit was safely underground in his burrow; and Baby Rook was swaying peacefully away high up in her tree-top.

And none of them ever suggested playing the 'All Change!' game again!

From *Country Bunch*

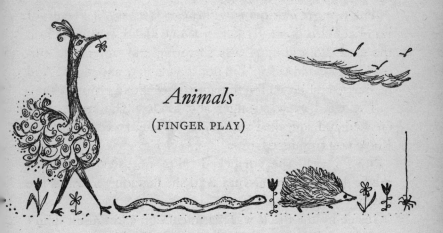

Animals

(FINGER PLAY)

Here is the ostrich straight and tall,
Nodding his head above us all.
  (*Stretch arm above head*)
Here is the long snake on the ground,
Wriggling upon the stones he found.
  (*Stretch arm horizontally and wriggle fingers*)
Here are the birds that fly so high,
Spreading their wings across the sky.
  (*Wave arms*)

Here is the hedgehog, prickly, small,
Rolling himself into a ball.
   (*Clench fist*)
Here is the spider scuttling round,
Treading so lightly on the ground.
   (*Move the fingers*)
Here are the children fast asleep,
   (*Pillow head on hands*)
And here at night the owls do peep.
   (*Circle eyes with thumb and forefinger*)

KATHLEEN BARTLETT

Birthday Soup

BY ELSE HOLMELUND MINARIK

'Mother Bear, Mother Bear, where are you?' calls Little Bear.

'Oh, dear, Mother Bear is not here, and today is my birthday. I think my friends will come, but I do not see a birthday cake. My goodness – no birthday cake. What can I do?

'The pot is by the fire. The water in the pot is hot. If I put something in the water, I can make Birthday Soup. All my friends like soup.

'Let me see what we have. We have carrots and potatoes, peas, and tomatoes; I can make soup with carrots, potatoes, peas, and tomatoes.'

So Little Bear begins to make soup in the big black pot. First, Hen comes in. 'Happy Birthday, Little Bear,' she says. 'Thank you, Hen,' says Little Bear.

Hen says, 'My! Something smells good here. Is it in the big black pot?'

'Yes,' says Little Bear, 'I am making Birthday Soup. Will you stay and have some?'

'Oh, yes, thank you,' says Hen. And she sits down to wait.

Next, Duck comes in. 'Happy Birthday, Little Bear,' says Duck. 'My, something smells good. Is it in the big black pot?'

'Thank you, Duck,' says Little Bear. 'Yes, I am making Birthday Soup. Will you stay and have some with us?'

'Thank you, yes, thank you,' says Duck. And she sits down to wait.

Next, Cat comes in. 'Happy Birthday, Little Bear,' he says.

'Thank you, Cat,' says Little Bear. 'I hope you like Birthday Soup. I am making Birthday Soup.'

Cat says, 'Can you really cook? If you can really make it, I will eat it.'

'Good,' says Little Bear. 'The Birthday Soup is hot, so we must eat it now. We cannot wait for Mother Bear. I do not know where she is.'

'Now, here is some soup for you, Hen,' says Little Bear. 'And here is some soup for you, Duck, and here is some soup for you, Cat, and here is some soup for me. Now we can all have some Birthday Soup.'

Cat sees Mother Bear at the door, and says, 'Wait, Little Bear. Do not eat yet. Shut your eyes, and say one, two, three.'

Little Bear shuts his eyes and says, 'One, two, three.' Mother Bear comes in with a big cake. 'Now, look,' says Cat.

'Oh, Mother Bear,' says Little Bear, 'what a big beautiful Birthday Cake! Birthday Soup is good to eat, but not as

good as Birthday Cake. I am so happy you did not forget.'

'Yes, Happy Birthday, Little Bear!' says Mother Bear. 'This Birthday Cake is a surprise for you. I never did forget your birthday, and I never will.'

From *Little Bear*

Tim Rabbit and the Scissors

BY ALISON UTTLEY

One day Tim Rabbit found a pair of scissors lying on the common. They had been dropped by somebody's mother, when she sat darning somebody's socks. Tim saw them shining in the grass, so he crept up very softly, just in case they might spring at him. Nearer and nearer he crept, but the scissors did not move, so he touched them with his whiskers, very gently, just in case they might bite him. He took a sniff at them, but nothing happened. Then he licked them, boldly, and, as the scissors were closed, he wasn't hurt. He admired the bright glitter of the steel, so he picked them up and carried them carefully home.

'Oh!' cried Mrs Rabbit, when he dragged them into the kitchen. 'Oh! Whatever's that shiny thing? A snake? Put it down, Tim!'

'It's a something I've found in the grass!' said Tim, proudly. 'It's quite tame.'

Mrs Rabbit examined the scissors, twisting and turning them, until she found that they opened and shut. She wisely put them on the table.

'We'll wait till your father comes home,' said she. 'He's gone to a meeting about the lateness of the swallows this year, but he said he wouldn't be long.'

'What have we here?' exclaimed Mr Rabbit when he returned.

'It's something Tim found,' said Mrs Rabbit, looking proudly at her son, and Tim held up his head and put his paws behind his back, just as his father did at a public meeting. Mr Rabbit opened the scissors and felt the sharp edges.

'Why! They're shears!' he cried, excitedly. 'They will trim the cowslip banks and cut the hay ready for the haystacks, when we gather our provender in the autumn.'

'Wait a minute!' he continued, snipping and snapping in the air. 'Wait a minute. I'll show you.' He ran out, carrying the scissors under his arm. In a few moments he came back with a neat bundle of grass, tied in a little sheaf.

'We can eat this in the peace and safety of our own house, by our own fireside, instead of sitting in the cold open fields,' said he. 'This is a wonderful thing you have found, Tim.'

Tim smiled happily, and asked, 'Will it cut other things, Father?'

'Yes, anything you like. Lettuces, lavender, dandelions, daisies, butter, and buttercups,' answered Mr Rabbit, but he put the scissors safely out of reach on a high shelf before he had his supper.

The next day, when his parents had gone to visit a neighbour, young Tim climbed on a stool and lifted down the bright scissors. Then he began to cut 'anything'.

First he snipped his little sheep's-wool blanket into bits, and then he snapped the leafy tablecloth into shreds. Next he cut into strips the blue window curtains which his mother had embroidered with gossamer threads, and then he spoilt the tiny roller-towel which hung behind the door. He turned his attention on himself, and trimmed his whiskers till nothing was left. Finally he started to cut off his fur. How delightful it was to see it drop in a flood of soft brown on the kitchen floor! How silky it was! He didn't know he had so much, and he clipped and clipped, twisting his neck and screwing round to the back, till the floor was covered with a furry fleece.

He felt so free and gay, so cool and happy, that he put the scissors away and danced lightly out of the room and on to the common like a dandelion-clock or a thistle-down.

Mrs Rabbit met him as she returned with her basket full of lettuces and little cabbage-plants, given to her by the kind neighbour, who had a garden near the village. She nearly fainted when she saw the strange white dancing little figure.

'Oh! Oh! Oh!' she shrieked. 'Whatever's this?'

'Mother, it's me,' laughed Tim, leaping round her like a newly-shorn lamb.

'No, it's not my Tim,' she cried sadly. 'My Tim is a fat fluffy little rabbit. You are a white rat, escaped from a menagerie. Go away.'

'Mother, it *is* me!' persisted Tim. 'It's Tim, your own Timothy Rabbit.' He danced and leaped over the basket which Mrs Rabbit had dropped on the ground.

'No! No! Go away!' she exclaimed, running into her house and shutting the door.

Tim flopped on the doorstep. One big tear rolled down his cheek and splashed on the grass. Then another and another followed in a stream.

'It *is* me,' he sobbed, with his nose against the crack of the door.

Inside the house Mrs Rabbit was gathering up the fur.

'It must have been Tim after all,' she sighed. 'This is his pretty hair. Oh, deary, deary me! Whatever shall I do?'

She opened the door. Tim popped his nose inside and sneezed.

'A-tishoo! A-tishoo! I'm so cold. A-tishoo! I won't do it again. I will be good,' he sniffed.

'Come in, young rabbit,' said Mrs Rabbit, severely. 'Get into bed at once, while I make a dose of hot camomile tea.'

But when Tim crept into bed there was no blanket. Poor Mrs Rabbit covered him with her own patchwork quilt, and then she gave him the hot posset.

'Now you must stay here till your fur grows again,' said she, and Tim lay underneath the red and blue patches of the bed-cover, thinking of the fun on the common, the leaping and galloping and turning somersaults of the little rabbits of the burrows, and he would not be there to join in.

Mr Rabbit was thoroughly shocked when he came home and saw his son, but he was a rabbit of ingenuity. He went out at once to borrow a spinning-wheel from an ancient rabbit who made coats to wrap Baby-Buntings in.

All day Mrs Rabbit wove the bits of fur, to make a little brown coat to keep Tim warm. When all the hairs were used up she pinned it round Tim with a couple of tiny sharp thorns from her pin-cushion.

'There you are, dressed again in your own fur,' said she, and she put a stitch here and there to make it fit.

How all the animals laughed when Tim ran out on the common, with his little white legs peeping out from the bottom of the funny short coat! How ashamed he was of his whiskerless face!

'Baa! Baa! White sheep! Have you any wool?' mocked his enemies the magpies, when he ran near the wall where they perched. But Tim's fur soon grew again, and then his troubles were over.

He hung his little coat on a gorse-bush for the chaffinches to take for their nests, and very glad they were to get it, too. As for the scissors, they are still lying on the high shelf, and you may see them if you peep down the rabbit hole on the edge of the common, where Tim Rabbit lives.

From *The Adventures of No Ordinary Rabbit*

Advice to a Child

Set your fir-tree
In a pot;
Needles green
Is all it's got.
Shut the door
And go away,
And so to sleep
Till Christmas Day.
In the morning
Seek your tree,
And you shall see
What you shall see.

Hang your stocking
By the fire,
Empty of
Your heart's desire;
Up the chimney
Say your say,
And so to sleep
Till Christmas Day.
In the morning
Draw the blind,
And you shall find
What you shall find.

ELEANOR FARJEON

Some other Young Puffins

THE ADVENTURES OF GALLDORA *Modwena Sedgwick*

ADVENTURES OF THE LITTLE WOODEN HORSE
Ursula Moray Williams

A BROTHER FOR THE ORPHELINES *Natalie Savage Carlson*

THE CASTLE OF YEW *Lucy Boston*

CLEVER POLLY AND THE STUPID WOLF
Catherine Storr

DANNY FOX *David Thomson**

DANNY FOX MEETS A STRANGER *David Thomson**

DEAR TEDDY ROBINSON *Joan G. Robinson*

FIVE DOLLS IN A HOUSE *Helen Clare*

GOBBOLINO THE WITCH'S CAT *Ursula Moray Williams*

THE HAPPY ORPHELINE *Natalie Savage Carlson*

LITTLE O *Edith Unnerstad*

LITTLE OLD MRS PEPPERPOT *Alf Prøysen*

LITTLE PETE STORIES *Leila Berg*

LITTLE RED FOX *Alison Uttley*

LUCKY DIP *Ruth Ainsworth*

MAGIC IN MY POCKET *Alison Uttley*

MEET MARY KATE *Helen Morgan*

THE MERRY-GO-ROUND *James Reeves*

MISS HAPPINESS AND MISS FLOWER *Rumer Godden*

* Young Puffin Originals

* Young Puffin Originals